# The Jester's Curse

## Run Amok

Hans Hergot

Bezzle Books
Columbia, South Carolina

Bezzle Books
1492 Lake Murray Boulevard
Columbia, South Carolina 29212

This is a work of fiction. Names, characters, places, and inci-
dents are a product of the author's imagination. Locales and
public names are sometimes used for atmospheric purposes.
Any resemblance to actual people, living or dead, or to busi-
nesses, companies, events, institutions, or locales is completely
coincidental.

Book Layout & Design courtesy of BookDesignTemplates.com

Ordering Information:
Quantity sales. Special discounts are available on quantity pur-
chases by corporations, associations, and others. For details,
contact the "Special Sales Department" at the address above.

The Jester's Curse: Run Amok / Hans Hergot. — 3d print ed.

# Prologue

Fire blazed from the lamps lining the walls of the banquet hall. They spun in the fool's vision as he turned round and round in the center of the room.

On the fool's back rode the master of the house, his face apoplectic. His hands reached out to strangle the fool.

Around the tangled pair, guests lined the well-appointed tables, watching the show. Already deep in their cups, the guests roared their approval of the fool's performance.

Guards wearing the light blue tunics of the house were less enthusiastic. They stood by, holding short swords, looking for an opportunity to assist their master.

When the piggy-back ride ended, the fool would be skewered. The guards couldn't miss him, dressed as he was in a quilt of riotous colors. And that was only if the master or the master's daughter didn't murder him first. He had sullied her honor. The father hadn't appreciated his joke; hence the homicidal maniac on his back.

The audience didn't know what to expect next. Neither did the fool. He had no control over his own body.

The fool had been cursed with a spell that made him an object of ridicule. The curse demanded that the fool make his audience laugh, no matter the cost. He bounced off chairs and tables, smashing his groin. The curse loved that joke above all others.

As his act built to its inevitable finale, and the guards readied their swords, the fool swore revenge on the wizard who had brought him to this ignominious fate—the wizard who had damned the fool by bestowing on him—the Jester's Curse.

# Chapter 1

## Four Months Earlier

Marius rounded the corner of the narrow corridor carrying a foul bucket. As a slave of House Cervix, Marius had been happy to accompany the family out of the cramped and crowded capitol of Zeno to the sprawling set of one story buildings that constituted their country residence.

Marius craned his neck away from the pot, trying to avoid the smell.

He was less happy about cleaning chamberpots. Still, that was his lot in life. And his masters weren't too bad.

House Cervix may not have been the greatest family in the Arovian Empire, but it enjoyed a good reputation among its slaves, who were treated as well as their station allowed.

Marius, a healthy looking boy of sixteen, had the black hair and eyes and olive skin that marked the native people of the Arovian peninsula. His nose had no bridge to speak of, but jutted directly out of his forehead. It would have been overlarge had Marius been thinner. But he had not suffered from malnourishment, not as a house slave.

Being born into slavery, though abject, came with certain privileges—like not starving to death. A physic would be called if he got sick, same as with any domesticated animal. The slaves of House Cervix always ate well, even Marius, the most junior boy in the house.

Marius moved quickly along the corridors, carrying a large copper bucket filled nearly to the brim with filthy water. The bucket contained the aftereffects of a hard night of drinking by one of the family's many guests.

Marius hurried to avoid being in the presence of the stench-filled bucket any longer than he had to be. His movements had the grace of someone caught between the need for speed and the need for balance. He didn't want a drop of the foul liquid to spill onto the red tunic that marked the family staff of House Cervix.

The rust-color of the tunic covered a multitude of sins. No one would notice if he spilled the filthy water on himself, but they might smell it. And he would certainly not be able to forget it.

Suddenly, a shadowy figure darted out of the doorway. Marius turned a pirouette, keeping the copper receptacle gripped tight to his chest.

"Soup of the day?" asked Sivinius.

Though four years older than Marius, Sivinius had yet to be promoted from his position as a house boy. Marius wasn't surprised.

In his usually unctuous voice, Sivinius added, "Careful now, a spill might ruin Flavorus's good mood."

Flavorus, the majordomo of the estate, was never in a good mood.

"Wouldn't want to trip you up." Sivinius stuck his feet in front of Marius's in quick succession.

Marius dodged the man's clumsy attempts to trip him. He managed to keep the chamberpot from overturning.

"Stop it!"

Marius had only lately moved into the ranks of the house slaves. On his arrival at the house, Sivinius had begun a campaign aimed at making Marius's life a living hell.

It was no wonder the man had never been promoted. Sivinius had nothing to recommend him: no looks to speak of, no pride in his work and even less skill. His penchant for gossip bested even the kitchen staff's.

Marius thought he could take Sivinius physically. But it was a capital crime to damage the property of an Arovian citizen, and both Sivinius and Marius were the property of House Cervix. Punching Sivinius in the face, no matter how good it might feel, would damage both Sivinius's face and Marius's hand. He would be liable for both.

Marius stopped moving. He couldn't risk spilling waste all over the corridor—not with all the guests on the estate and not with the entire family there as well.

None of the slaves—except Flavorus and possibly Sivinius, given how much he gossiped—knew why the house was flooded with guests or why the entire family had retired to the country.

The slaves knew it must be important but had been almost too busy to speculate, except for Sivinius. He'd been ordered to help Marius clean the guest's room that morning but, as usual, was nowhere to be found.

Marius chalked it up to Sivinius's usual laziness but wondered whether Sivinius knew from experience what awaited them in that chamber and had left Marius to do the dirty work.

"Don't you wish you knew what I knew?" said Sivinius. He leaned against a wall with his legs crossed and a hand on his hip.

Sivinius had already let a few meaty hints drop about the special guests. He waited for Marius to take the bait.

Marius had no intention of obliging the man. Sivinius never told the whole story or would leave off right before an important part. Begging and cajoling might get the rest out of him, or it might not. Bribery worked better. Marius refused to engage Sivinius if he could help it.

"There's going to be an announcement soon." Sivinius examined the back of his nails. "Did you know that a magician from the White Tower is coming to the house? What do you say to that?"

Marius said nothing. He showed neither encouragement nor disdain. Either expression would have satisfied the other's need for attention, and neither Marius's contempt nor goodwill would alter the way Sivinius treated him.

"A magician from the White Tower to perform some spells. And the head of House Polonius arrived last night. House Polonius and House Cervix under the same roof. Whatever could it mean?" Sivinius smiled, but his good humor, if it could be called such, did not include Marius.

"We are moving up in the world," said Sivinius. "There will be a merger. As with all mergers some survive and others do not."

Marius finally responded, "Spit it out already."

"I need something from you, Marius," said Sivinius. "A favor."

Marius waited for a few smelly seconds for the request that was coming.

Frustration began to build. He could endure Sivinius all day and night—and he had to, since they shared duties and a room together. But he couldn't take both the putrescence of man and the gag-inducing chamber pot at the same time.

The thought occurred to him that Sivinius had been lying in wait on Marius to emerge with the chamberpot, figuring that he'd be eager to agree so that he could get on with the dirty job. If so, Sivinius had figured wrong.

"I want," said Sivinius, "to serve the guest table tonight."

"Flavorus makes the assignments," said Marius. He responded automatically, relieved not to have to capitulate to what was essentially a demand.

"You could make something up. Tell him you were not feeling well or that your back ached," said Sivinius.

Marius tried to put the pieces together—to think why Sivinius wanted to wait on the guest table as opposed to his usual place at the side of the master's wife and her mother. The older woman especially doted on Sivinius.

In the end, it came down to the fact that Marius simply didn't trust Sivinius and had no intention of doing him any favors, not after how Sivinius had treated him.

"Take it up with Flavorus."

"Are you sure? You might regret your decision later."

The tone in Sivinius's voice reminded Marius that he had to close his eyes sometime. The room they shared was going to be awfully tense that night.

"Sivinius, you've earned as many favors from me as a pagan at prayers."

Sivinius shrugged, stepping out of Marius's path. "Have it your way."

Resuming his journey down the corridors, Marius wondered how Sivinius intended to pay him back.

He stepped into a sunlit courtyard and tripped. Marius tried to juggle the bucket, but it and the murky contents that it contained overturned, spilled over him and the stone-tiled courtyard.

Covered in filth, Marius looked to see what had tripped him. His eyes adjusted to the sunlight. A stool lay on its side in the doorway. It had been put there on purpose.

Sivinius appeared, leaning on the doorway emitting a particularly high giggle that grated so badly on Marius's nerves. Sivinius again examined his fingernails as if any dirt could attach to someone so habitually lazy.

"It's too bad you didn't want to be friendly. I could have warned you about this stool." He righted the piece of wood with his foot absentmindedly.

Blood rushed to Marius's face. His eyes went red with anger. Sivinius had placed the stool in the doorway, knowing Marius would not be able to see it, not with the sun and the large chamber pot blocking his view. Marius rose with his fists clenched.

Sivinius strode forward, his chin sticking out. "Something you want to do, Marius? Go ahead." His sneer invited a blow. It took all of Marius's strength not to strike out.

"By the Lady, Sivinius—"

"Language, language," said Sivinius. "House Polonius brought a priest with them. What if he heard the name of his goddess coming out of your filthy mouth?"

Footsteps echoed from the other side of the courtyard. Marius looked in horror at the opposite entrance and back at Sivinius—only to discover that he'd disappeared, as he always did at the first sign of work or trouble.

If only Marius had been so prepared or so experienced, he wouldn't be the one looking into the shocked eyes of Flavorus, the majordomo of House Cervix, as he led the guests back to their rooms after having broken their fast.

Flavorus took one look at Marius and at the courtyard before altering course. The guests would be taking the scenic route. Marius would be getting a beating. And his best tunic was ruined.

In the short time since he'd been promoted to a house slave, Marius had not complained at Sivinius's abuse. But a line had finally been crossed.

Later that morning, as the straps of Flavorus's whip found a sharp home on Marius's bare back, he swore to repay Sivinius. He would do it before the day was out and in a way that would guarantee Sivinius never bothered him again.

# Chapter 2

Dinner time found Marius cleaned up and in his second best tunic awaiting the family and guests. Flavorus stood behind the head table. The overseer gave him a bracing glare.

Marius's back ached from the beating. Blood trickled down his back. He resisted the urge to touch it. Injured or not, Marius had a night of hard work ahead of him. He focused on the task at hand, scanning the table to make sure every fork, every glass was in its proper place.

A total of twenty slaves waited on the family and its guests to arrive. Twenty was a sufficient number of slaves as befitted the prominence of House Cervix and the importance of the rich guests from House Polonius.

Marius had heard that the slaves of Polonius, dressed in their rich purple tunics, had offered to help with the dinner service. Marius would have welcomed the assistance. He might even have gotten out of the duty. But Flavorus, proud as ever, would not hear of it.

Flavorus was a stickler for decorum. And he never wasted workers on frivolities. He considered dinner service to be light work, almost a vacation from their usual chores, never mind that the duty could last all night and that if a slave was attractive or a guest too drunk, it might require something more than most slaves would freely give.

Marius himself had never been propositioned, either because of his young age or his hawkish nose. In fact, Flavorus, as a rule, did not allow handsome slaves in the house—which was not a bad policy and might explain in part the continued presence of Sivinius.

The oily eyes of his enemy stared at Marius from behind the women's table. Sivinius stuck his thumb between his fingers, surreptitiously showing Marius the rude gesture.

Sivinius had not succeeded in getting Marius's duty with the guests. Marius was glad for that small victory, though serving the women might have been less rigorous on his back. At least the rust-colored tunic of House Cervix would hide the fresh blood that was slowly turning into scabs.

The family and guests began the procession from the inner chambers where they had taken light refreshment and drinks. Their pace was slow and had the appearance of being casual. To the experienced observer, it was anything but. The order of entrance was strictly observed, the master and wife proceeded a few paces in front of the mother-in-law who, in her own house, would go first but who, in her daughter's husband's house, must give way.

Had House Cervix been of sufficiently high rank so as not to care what any of the guests thought, the married children and their spouses would have followed with the unmarried sons and daughters bringing up the rear. But it was not.

And so, the children of House Cervix waited obsequiously on the more important guests of House Polonius who might one day hold it in their power to bestow some privilege. The children of House Cervix waited too on the wizard from the White Tower.

The mage was the last of the guests to enter the dining room. The others had already reclined on low sofas with tables within easy reach when the man of magic entered the room.

The magician was accompanied by a man dressed in black leather armor with a red star painted on the breastplate. Marius recognized the sign of the Astors, the appointed guardians of the Kingdom of Arovia. Astors were a law unto themselves and answered only to the Emperor.

Marius hadn't heard that an Astor would be join-
ing the family for dinner, but perhaps the man had
only lately arrived. The dust on his black leather
boots certainly seemed to indicate that the Astor
had traveled from the road directly to the dining
hall. The man's cloak fluttered as he walked, revealing a wicked -looking dagger hanging from his belt.
His eyes never stopped moving around the room.
They landed briefly on Marius.

Something about those eyes troubled the young
slave. Though the Astor's face was otherwise handsome, the eyes were set too close together to inspire trust.

The family and the guests apparently took no
notice of the two men, but Marius was certain that
the wizard and the Astor occupied the peripheral
vision of all in the room including the slaves. Sivinius, in particular, ran a hand through his slick, black
hair and smiled—his malevolent gaze at Marius
forgotten for the moment.

The mage wore a long white robe. He did not
look particularly imposing or distinguished, but his
eyes seemed to capture the fire of every candle in
the room and his nose was as crooked as a broken
toe.

The children of House Cervix slunk in after the
wizard and took whichever seats were left. The entire party had situated itself without conscious effort or communication into a natural arrangement

honoring power and influence. This, according to Flavorus, was a sign of good breeding.

Dinner service began without ceremony. House Cervix was not religious. No prayers were raised, much to the consternation of a priest who had entered with House Polonius and who sought quietly, with head bowed, to rectify the omission.

Marius noted that when the priest looked up, he found himself staring into the eyes of the wizard. Marius, who had heard stories about the bad blood between wizards and priests, waited to see what happened next. The wizard nodded with a wry smile in the priest's direction. The priest, more discomfited by this development than by the lack of a formal prayer, suddenly became very busy arranging his utensils.

Marius returned his gaze to the tables around him, seeking to fill any empty glasses just as the first course came from the kitchen: platters full of baked mice.

Between courses, Marius listened to the chatter of the other slaves. It seemed that the head of House Polonius had arrived with his fifth son. Speculation ran rampant that a match was being arranged for one of the unwed daughters of House Cervix. The priest, then, might be there to bless the union, and the wizard there for a more practical purpose, to ensure that the wedding night was fruitful. Several of the serving girls tittered at that suggestion.

Even Marius, who didn't have a head for politics, recognized it as an even match on both sides. House Polonius was more highly esteemed than House Cervix, but they offered, after all, only their fifth son.

Sivinius must have figured all this out long ago and sought to ingratiate himself with the guests from House Polonius in anticipation of the so-called "merger" as he had put it. That explained his interest in serving at the guest table. Sivinius wanted a position with the new family.

Marius, for his part, was content to serve House Cervix for the rest of his life, just as his parents had done. He hoped one day to fill Flavorus's position as majordomo. But for the moment, he was looking for a way to spite Sivinius. So far, nothing had come to mind.

Marius focused instead on the dinner service and on trying to arrange his posture so that his tunic came into contact with his tattered back as infrequently as possible.

Picking up a silver tray filled with the tiny discarded bones of the mice, Marius hurried back to the kitchen.

He swerved around the busy cooks, dodging elbows and knives. The kitchen seemed a thing of constant motion as cooks stirred pots before removing them from the fire and ladling their steaming contents onto tiny plates or large bowls. The bustle was a welcome break from the staid formal dinner. Marius relaxed.

Dumping the bones into a slop bucket, he handed the silver tray to the washing girl. Her smile shone through the remains of dinner that covered her face, hands, and clothing. Marius almost envied her. The girl had no other concerns outside of the rote task set before her. She didn't have to put on a show for the fancy dinner guests.

Marius slumped against a table, taking some of the weight off his tired feet. He touched gingerly at his back pulling his tunic away from the wounds in order to keep the rough fabric from attaching to the scabs that were forming.

Over the noise of the kitchen a voice called out, "Hey, you! No loafing."

Marius's head swiveled, looking for his accuser.

A cook dressed in the rust colored tunic of House Cervix pushed her way through the busy kitchen toward Marius. She wiped her hand on a well-used apron before wagging a finger at him.

Marius's face broke into a grin.

"By the Lady, Agestah, I thought you were Flavorus."

"If I had been," she said, "you'd be in for it." Agestah came to rest on the table beside Marius. The plump, shorter woman had to look up at him. She brushed aside a stray strand of auburn hair.

Marius tried to smile, but it came out more as a grimace, "I don't think he could beat me again without killing me."

"Don't think he won't try."

Though Agestah smiled back, Marius noted the lines of worry radiating from her eyes. Agestah was the closest thing he had to family since the plague had taken his parents. Marius didn't want to be a cause for concern.

"Anyhow," said Agestah, "come by after dinner and I'll get you something to put on your back."

"I'd rather you got me something to put in my stomach."

"That too," Agestah smiled. "How about for now we settle for putting something in those shiftless hands of yours." Reaching behind her on the table, Agestah picked up a basket of bread and shoved it toward Marius.

Agestah had been teasing him about lazing around, but only just. In her own way, the head cook was as demanding as Flavorus. Marius, taking the hint, began to rise. He reached for the basket.

She held him in place. "Watch yourself, Marius. I heard Sivinius has it in for you."

If anyone could be counted on to have heard the house gossip, it was the kitchen staff and their boss, Agestah.

"Tell me something I don't know," said Marius. Sivinius had been hounding him ever since Marius became a member of the house staff.

"This is something different. I'm not sure what you did to him, but—"

"Dared to exist," Marius blurted out.

Agestah sighed. "That's as may be," she said. "Still, you want to watch yourself while the important guests are here."

Marius nodded, gratefully accepting the basket of bread and the advice. He would be on guard against Sivinius. Better yet, if Marius could help it, he would beat the odious slave at his own game.

\* \* \*

By the time Marius returned to the dining hall, the lamps and candles had been lit. As with all important dinners, it was going to be a long affair. Marius steeled himself against the inevitable.

His eyes soon glazed over with the look of one long accustomed to his duty, till something unusual caught Marius's attention.

Sivinius bent over to pour wine into the mother-in-law's goblet. As he did, the front of his rust-colored tunic came near an open candle.

It happened again. Then again. Marius held his breath as Sivinius's shirt slipped a finger's breadth from the candle's burning wick.

Sivinius seemed intent on saving Marius the trouble of taking revenge. If the man caught himself on fire, what ridicule, what punishment would follow?

The event played itself out in Marius's mind. It brought a smile to his face to think of his enemy running around the room on fire. Suddenly, the lashes on his back didn't hurt nearly as much.

Each time Sivinius neared the open flame, Marius agonized. He blew heavily out of his mouth, willing the flame to move closer, near enough for combustion.

Yet the glorious conflagration never happened. By sheer luck, Sivinius managed to avoid danger each time. The suspense drove Marius to distraction. He wasn't performing his best dinner service. A prickling glance from Flavorus confirmed this; yet, for once, Marius didn't care.

Each time Sivinius passed the candle, hope sprang up in Marius's heart. Each time Sivinius passed unscathed, Marius lost faith in the world.

Finally, the thought occurred to Marius, during the seventh course of the meal, that fate might need a helping hand. If the candle were moved closer to the edge of the table—

Marius knew the tunic would burn at the merest touch of a flame. He'd seen it happen before and had taken the warning to heart. Their clothing burned more easily than a twig.

The next time Marius's pitcher went dry, he did not go directly to the kitchen. He walked by the table Sivinius was serving. Marius leaned over, moving the mother-in-law's candle nearer the table's edge. While the old woman was otherwise engaged, Marius tipped her wine glass into his empty pitcher. He walked to the door and paused inside, waiting to see what would happen.

Sivinius, who had been out of the room, returned to find the old woman's glass empty. He stared at it in puzzlement. Finally, Sivinius moved alongside the woman, bending over to fill her cup.

The effect was immediate. The tip of his tunic touched the candle. It burst into flames. Sivinius lurched, spilling wine on the old woman.

The majordomo, Flavorus, rushed at Sivinius, waving his arms. Sivinius, scared of the fire and of Flavorus's looming presence, ran into the middle of the room where he spun in a circle, beating out the flame with one hand while the other, outstretched with the pitcher, showered wine on all of the guests including the Astor and the wizard.

Flavorus caught Sivinius and threw him forcefully to the ground, rubbing him back and forth as though rolling up a difficult carpet.

With the flame extinguished, Flavorus pulled Sivinius to his feet and shook him as a dog shakes a rat. Sivinius looked terrified.

"What have you done, you fool?" Flavorus's voice carried over the quiet crowd. They were as anxious as Marius to see how the drama would unfold. If it were exciting enough—say, ending with Sivinius's death—they might forgive having their clothes ruined by the red wine.

Sivinius wailed, "I don't know!"

A slave stepped forward, a fat girl named Orsa, one of Sivinius's confidants. Marius wondered what she might possibly be thinking interfering at a time like this. Was it possible that anyone would defend Sivinius?

She pointed directly at Marius instead. "He did it."

Marius struggled to breathe.

Sivinius gasped. "He said he would get back at me! He blamed me for that mess in the courtyard. And now this?"

A tear welled up in the serving girl's eye. "I saw him move the candle. He was so jealous of me and Sivinius. I never thought anyone could be so wicked." She fled the room.

They were lying. None of that stuff had ever happened.

Marius tried to speak but found he could not. His defense lodged in his throat. True, he had moved the candle, but he'd never looked twice at that girl before.

Flavorus was staring at him, seething. Behind Flavorus's back, Sivinius set his face in a subtle smirk.

Sivinius had set him up. He must have known that Marius would be looking for revenge. Sivinius had provided a convenient opportunity and an eyewitness as well. He must've offered the girl something, a pastry perhaps.

Flavorus marched with purpose toward Marius, looking as though he intended to beat Marius to death with his bare hands in front of the entire party, who might actually approve the rough justice.

From their perspective, it would be proper recompense for their ruined clothing.

Marius felt his legs go weak. His life was forfeit.

"Stop!" A figure rose from a table, halting Flavorus with an outstretched hand.

Flavorus shrunk away. Marius wondered what force on earth could have made the majordomo back down. Then he saw who had risen, and his heart quailed.

The Astor stood. He reached for the dagger that hung from his belt.

"No, my friend. Do not trouble yourself. Allow me," said the wizard.

His white robes swirled as he rose from his seat. The wizard locked eyes with Marius, who could not look away.

# Chapter 3

H e is guilty," the wizard proclaimed. "I can see it in his eyes."

The crowd mumbled. The Astor took his seat.

Marius hardly knew what to say. He began to protest, to plead his innocence—well not exactly innocence.

The wizard preempted his plea. "He likes to make jokes, this one?" With his hand, he indicated Marius, but the wizard's eyes lingered on the priest, issuing an unspoken challenge, waiting to see if the priest would object. When he did not, the wizard shrugged, looking almost disappointed. "This slave likes to make jokes. So I will make a joke on him."

The wizard waved his hand and said a few words in an unknown tongue. The priest's face went white. He put two fingers to his chest in the sigh of a ward and pushed them toward Marius as though Marius's very presence was blasphemous.

The wizard sat down and resumed his meal.

Marius felt something inside himself give—as though someone had reached into him like a trussed bird and broken his wishbone leaving him with the short end.

He couldn't begin to comprehend what had happened. Everyone was watching to see if the ruin of their best clothes would be worth it. Perhaps they expected Marius to melt or to explode or to grow gigantic ears and a tail like a donkey.

For his part, Marius didn't know what he was supposed to do. He hadn't turned to dust or into a frog. None of the old stories about wizards speculated much beyond those outcomes.

Finally, he started to speak, "Wh-wh-what happened?" He stuttered. The pitch of his voice was all wrong, alternating from deep bass to high squeaks.

The dinner crowd began to snigger. Marius sounded like an idiot.

Unhindered now by the Astor, Flavorus resumed his march toward Marius with both fists clenched.

Marius had already taken one beating. Another might kill him, especially given the look in Flavorus's eyes.

Marius took a step back. Then two things happened simultaneously. The pitcher he was carrying slipped. He spilled its contents down the front of his pants. And Marius fell backwards, landing on the top of his tailbone.

"Ow-ow-ow!" Marius's face twisted in pain.

The crowd roared its approval. They found him ridiculous.

Flavorus reached Marius and grabbed at his tunic. Marius slipped out of his grip like a wet fish, falling back to the cold, stone floor.

Marius tried to get up. He fell again. Flavorus's arms were around his neck, then under his armpit. Yet, again and again he fell.

The more times Marius fell, the harder the crowd laughed. The slaves joined in. Sivinius slapped his thigh, his high-pitched laugh warbled over the crowd.

Flavorus finally gave up. He moved Marius offstage by a series of kicks to the backside, each of which was met by uproarious laughter.

Neither Marius nor Flavorus joined in the mirth. Marius cried as each blow sent shocks up his already-marred back. Flavorus, whether he knew it or not, played the role of the straight man better than anyone in history.

In the courtyard, Flavorus stood Marius against a post. He found the whip already in his hand thanks to Sivinius. He let the lash fly.

Flavorus missed. The whip cracked, severing the cord supporting Marius's pants.

His pants fell. At that instant, Marius farted.

The slaves who'd come to witness Marius's death laughed.

Throwing his hands to the sky, Flavorus gave up. He gave orders for Marius to be thrown out of the estate. It took four slaves to carry him, each grabbing a hand or a foot. Sivinius led the procession.

Marius squirmed, but he couldn't escape their grasp.

Being exiled from the house was a fate nearly worse than being beaten to death and only slightly less gristly.

It wasn't the same as being set free. Marius would still be a slave, marked by dress and manner as another person's property.

No one would help him. He would be left to die of hunger or exposure like a wounded wild beast. Or wicked men might take him. Or the army might use him for target practice.

There were a thousand ways he could die—and no one—not even Marius—believed he would live for long outside House Cervix.

The heavy gate closed behind him, sealing his fate.

# Chapter 4

The afternoon sun beat down on Marius's neck. A fly buzzed by his ear. He became suddenly alert, the way one does when awaking in an unfamiliar setting.

The ground beneath his head was a great deal harder than his normal sleeping mat, the sky above him so much wider than the tiny room he shared with Sivinius, the leaves of the tree under which he lay so much greener than the walls of the Cervix estate.

As his mind awoke to the new day, memories of the night before burned through Marius's head. His cheeks flushed.

Marius tried to stand up, but his legs fell out from under him, as though they had a mind of their own. Finally, clutching the trunk of the tree, Marius managed to raise himself to his feet.

He glanced around. The walls surrounding the country estate of House Cervix lay only a stone's throw away. Marius hadn't made it far before collapsing under the weight of the beatings he'd endured and the despair that welled up in his heart.

Looking around the surrounding countryside, Marius took no pleasure in the rolling hills or the blue sky.

He'd never slept till past noon before. In fact, he hadn't slept past sunrise since he was a little boy. But even the late hour of his waking, as late as the most dissipated noble, gave him no pleasure.

He didn't know what to do with himself. He was so used to taking orders.

Marius realized he had nothing to do, nowhere to go. He didn't even know where "here" was. The family and their slaves had only recently exchanged the capital city of Zeno for the country. It was Marius's first visit to the estate.

He looked at the large wooden gates waiting for something to happen, for someone to let him back in, for someone to say it had all been some huge misunderstanding.

As he watched, a devil's door built into the larger gate swung open. A male slave hurried out, carrying a large wicker basket, going to secure produce from the local village.

Marius called out, "H-h-hello!"

The man didn't even pause. Marius had known him his entire life. They had literally slaved away together. Now, nothing. He stared at the man's back as he walked down the road, vaguely aware that he himself must take that same path.

"You still here then?"

Marius's head snapped toward the door.

"Ag-g-gestah!"

The diminutive woman stepped through the small door. She held in her hand a similar basket to the one the slave had been carrying.

The sunlight caught her auburn hair. Marius suddenly wished that time would stop, that he could stay in this moment forever.

She wagged a finger at him, "What if Flavorus comes around?"

"What's he g-going to d-do?"

"You might not feel that way when you're dead!" Agestah laid a small hand on his chest.

Point in fact, Marius wouldn't feel anything at all if he were dead. That peaceful state of rest seemed eminently preferable to the uncertainty roiling within him.

Agestah put her hand to his cheek, examining his face. "What happened to you?"

Marius shrugged, "Ask the w-wizard."

The gentle clucking of her tongue demonstrated Agestah's disapproval. "You've got to leave, get out of here. I packed you a basket."

"N-no." Marius clenched his fists. "I want S-sivinius first."

"Forget about him," she said. "What if you did get him? You'd be killed for damaging house property. Not that he's liable to step outside those gates while you're around."

"J-just let me th-think."

Marius glanced down the road toward the green hills. He would have to tell his feet to walk away from all that he had ever known to a place where he was neither known nor welcome. As an outcast slave, he had no protection.

Where would he go? What would he do? His thoughts ran ahead of them so fast that he had no chance to answer. Before his mind uttered a question, a hundred more were in its place.

Being raised as a slave came with certain advantages. Food and clothing were provided into old age. No one could touch you without fear of damaging a wealthy man's property. But slavery also came with a price.

Marius felt dumb as a donkey. He knew nothing of surviving in the country. As a young boy, he'd played in the streets of Zeno. He knew the area around the capital city well. The country, on the other hand, was a mystery.

Even if he wanted to go back to the city, he simply didn't know the way. He thought about going back—after all, the slaves in the city couldn't possibly have heard about his dismissal—he'd have at least a week till word traveled back.

Yet it wasn't as though he could ask anyone for directions to Zeno. There was his stupid stutter to contend with, and he would be treated as a runaway slave, despite the fact that it had never been his intention to leave.

Marius looked at his hands as if there was something they were supposed to be doing.

When he'd left Zeno for the first time, there had been all the excitement of travel and seeing the world, even though it was just a short trip from the city to the country estate. Now, Marius felt a deep sense of foreboding.

Marius said quietly, "I don't know what to do. Tell me what I should do."

Agestah smiled sadly. "How can a slave tell a free man what to do?"

Free. Marius hardly knew the word.

"But if it was me," said Agestah, "I'd go to Amok."

"Amok?"

Agestah looked wistfully into the distance, "I grew up there, worked for a wonderful family, House Marcel, till they sold me."

Marius's mouth hung open. He'd never heard anything about this from Agestah or from his parents. He'd known the woman practically all his life.

"Sold you? Why?"

Agestah sighed, "Had their reasons, I suppose, but it was hard, especially being separated from— But look at me blathering on while you've got a journey to take."

"Agestah—"

"Go to Amok. The majordomo's name there is Yavont. He should remember me, though it's been more than fifteen years. Find Yavont. Tell him I sent you. He'll take care of you. Now go, before Flavorus find you or, worse, the wizard or that Astor that's with him."

"But—"

"Find Yavont. House Marcel is a rich house. He might even be able to help you find a cure for your curse."

A cure? Marius hadn't even thought such a thing might be possible. Hope stirred within him.

A new voice inserted itself into the conversation, "Leaving so soon?"

Marius turned toward the gate. There, in the bolt hole, was the ugly face of his tormentor, Sivinius.

"I'm sorry to see you go!" said Sivinius.

"You'll b-b-be sorry all right!" Marius stuttered. He couldn't help it.

"What was that?" Sivinius put a hand to his ear in a mock gesture of confusion.

Come closer, thought Marius, and I'll tell you: right to your smug face.

Outwardly, he said nothing.

"I got a promotion, by the way," Sivinius gloated. "It never would have happened without you!"

Marius had had enough of the insipid man. He picked up a rough-looking rock, took a step, and threw it at the door. He didn't expect to hit Sivinius, but there was always a chance.

As he released the rock, Marius felt his fingers slip. Instead of chucking the rock at the gate, it flew a straight into the air. Marius looked up just in time to see the stone hurtling at his head. He scrunched his brow, protecting his eyes, but his forehead took a sharp blow. He knew without checking that he was bleeding.

Sivinius giggled. "Oh that was good. Try again!" He clapped his hands in front of his sharp nose, resting his fingers on his lips.

Whatever the wizard had done to Marius had made a mess of his reflexes. His mouth no longer worked. And he couldn't trust his body.

Marius couldn't even tell Sivinius to go to the dogs. He stuck his thumb between his fingers and pointed the rude gesture at Sivinius.

Only, it was no longer Sivinius's face at the bolt hole.

Flavorus was staring out, and he looked livid.

Flavorus called to the guards. The door to the estate swung open. Men with swords rushed out.

But Marius was already moving down the lane in a full sprint. He could have sworn over his pumping legs and racing heart that he heard Sivinius's high, girlish laugh drifting over the fields.

His last sight was of Agestah waving after him, still holding the basket.

# Chapter 5

Marius wasn't sure whether it was the off-pitch whistling or the splatter of urine landing near his head that woke him. Going to sleep—more like passing out—hungry as he was, Marius wasn't convinced that he would ever wake again.

He blinked and put a hand to his eyes, shielding himself from the sun and from the splatter. Sick as his body was, the outrageousness of getting peed on was enough to rouse him from his stupor.

"Wh-wh-what are you doing?"

"Ah. He's alive?"

The man's voice sounded strange, and his costume as he came into focus was even stranger. His dark face was a mass of wrinkles outlined by a patchy beard. He was covered, shoulder to knee, by a shift of rough, plain wool, tied at the waist by a bright sash. A wrap covered his head but was not enough to contain the long hair that fell down over his shoulders. The hair was black, but heavy and gray at the tips.

"Poking a dead man with a stick . . . not so pleasant," said the man. "A little whiz does the job and clears my bladder at the same time."

"Wh-wh-who are you?"

"I am Asadal the Walker. Who are you?"

"Marius." Thankfully he didn't stutter.

"I see, I see, but what are you?" Asadal tapped on Marius's ribs with a long, thin stick.

"Thought you didn't p-p-poke people."

"Don't poke dead people. You aren't dead." Again, the man's accent threw Marius a bit. Growing up in Zeno, the great metropolis, strange faces from foreign lands were not uncommon. Yet, Asadal's face and his speech were stranger than most.

Asadal continued. "Close to dead, but not dead. Sit up."

Marius, so used to obeying, complied.

Marius had been chased away from the village near the Cervix estate. Not only had he received no help from the villagers, they stood by and watched as their children chased him down the road throwing rocks. They clapped when one scored a hit.

Marius had hoped that the color of his tunic, as a slave of House Cervix, might earn him some respect from the villagers. However, the slave that had gone to fetch vegetables must have warned the villagers about Marius, the disgraced ex-slave.

They had been on guard against him. Eyes were on him from the moment he arrived lest he take it into his head to try to steal.

Marius hadn't had the good sense to enter the village by cover of night, seeing as he'd been chased by heavily armed guards, who thankfully tired of sprinting in heavy armor.

The wizard's curse only made him trip once during the chase. The guards had been too grim to laugh.

Marius left town hungry and, worse, thirsty and, even more tragically, with no clue how to alleviate either symptom.

Three days later, he'd lain down by the side of the road. He hadn't done it intending to die. He was tired of being hungry, tired of being thirsty.

Still, he sat up at Asadal's insistence.

"Take this." Asadal put a flagon into Marius's hands.

It was marvelously squishy in his grip. He put the end into his mouth and drank. He could actually taste the water with all the wonderful minerals of the ground it was pulled from.

"Slow. Slow. Careful."

Marius was amazed that the curse let him drink without spilling the water down his front. Then Marius choked. His stomach rebelled. He leaned forward, puking everything he'd swallowed back onto the dusty ground.

"Try again. Slowly."

Marius again took a pull at the flagon. The taste was not as sweet this time, tainted as it was by the bile still coating his throat.

Asadal sat down on a large rock beside Marius. He watched and waited as Marius slowly drained the flagon.

"S-s-sorry," said Marius, "I drank it all."

"No problem, son," said Asadal. "There's a stream not a moment's walk that-a-way." He motioned with his pointy stick. Marius wondered what the stick was for. It was hardly thick enough to take the man's weight, and anyone who meant the man serious harm would simply laugh at it. But it was the mention of the stream that really caught his attention.

"A stream?"

"Yes, you know, trickling water?" Asadal made a swerving motion with one hand.

Marius nodded. He knew what a stream was. They'd crossed a few during the trip to the Cervix estate. They'd gone over a stone bridge that spanned a rushing river. To think that, with water so close, he'd almost died of thirst.

Maybe that was the curse's idea of a joke. Marius found it bitterly ironic.

Asadal eyed Marius. "You got some bad spell on you, son. And yet—"

Marius touched his chest instinctively, as though he was wearing the curse on his tunic. "Y-y-you can see it?"

"Something strange about that curse. Something I can't quite put my finger on. But I think we can do something about the stutter, eh?" Asadal reached down. Plucking a thin piece of grass between two dark fingers, he broke it into sections and braided them, connecting them at the end with a small bob. "Put this on your finger."

Marius raised an eyebrow. The piece of grass didn't look like anything.

"I got a little magic. Try and see."

With nothing to lose but his pride should it be some kind of joke, Marius took the grass ring and slipped it onto his finger. It fit snugly and would not budge over his knuckle. He tried it instead on his smallest finger.

"There now. Don't you feel better?"

In fact, Marius felt nothing at all. When the wizard had cursed him, it had felt like his insides were bending. He didn't feel any uncoiling at the touch of the grass.

"I don't think it works," said Marius.

He stared at the ring with his mouth wide open. He hadn't stuttered.

"Careful, you'll catch flies."

Marius was so hungry that he would have eaten any fly dumb enough to enter his mouth.

As though sensing the ex-slave's thoughts, Asadal pulled a piece of bread from a place inside his shift, handing it to Marius, who hardly stopped to wonder where it had come from, seeing as the shift seemed to lack pockets.

Marius ate the bread bite by bite. It was difficult to control his appetite, but he didn't want to vomit again nor cherished the prospect of having to eat the vomit if he did indeed puke, which he would have done to recover any regurgitated nutrients. Thankfully, the bread did not reappear.

As he ate, a cart drove by pulled by oxen. The driver eyed them cautiously; then, deciding that the old man and the gaunt slave weren't a threat, he ignored them entirely.

Asadal called out, "A coin? A coin for a Walker?"

"Go to the Lady!" replied the driver.

"I did," said Asadal, "She said you were in arrears and that I should collect for her."

"You Walkers are a pestilence to the road. Lay down in front of my cart. I'll give you a coin for that."

"Ah, but then I would owe you when my stout body broke your cart."

The driver laughed, "You've got a smart tongue, Walker, and for that I won't stop to beat you."

"Then you'll have to take my tongue lashing your back as you drive away."

The cart was now well past the stone on which Asadal sat. He called after the man, "May your travels be hot and your women cold!"

The driver did not respond audibly but raised a fist with a thumb tucked into his fingers.

Asadal the Walker shook his head, smiling. He looked over at Marius.

"Too bad he wasn't going our way. I think I could have gotten us a ride."

"Our way?"

"I'm on my way to Amok. Ever been there? A big city like that. Lots of chances for a young man like you."

Amok. Hadn't Agestah told him to go there and find Yavont, the majordomo of House Marcel?

Asadal slapped and rubbed at his knees. "Now I have helped you. You must help Asadal."

Marius gulped down last bite of bread. He didn't know what the man wanted, but he was on the hook for whatever it was. The man had saved his life.

Asadal smiled, his white teeth set off by his otherwise swarthy complexion, "Tell me your story."

It wasn't much to ask. But Marius's story was the sort of thing that a bad person might use against him. Yet he hadn't gotten the impression that Asadal was a bad person. Not that he seemed a good person either.

Marius recounted what had happened. How he was cursed by the magician and kicked out of the household, and how he had come to lie down by the side of the road only to be awoken by the sound of Asadal's morning ablutions.

"And lucky you were that I have a small bladder," said Asadal. "But did you have no one to speak up for you?"

"My parents are dead. It's just me."

"Ah, I'm sorry, Marius." Asadal put a hand on the boy's shoulder. The strong grip felt comforting.

After a moment, Asadal continued. "The magician who put a spell on you, what did he say exactly?"

"He said that, because I like to make jokes, he would make me a joke."

Asadal nodded soberly. His fingers pulled at his lower lip.

"Since then, have funny things been happening?"

Marius nodded. "Especially when I'm around other people."

"That's it then."

"What is?"

"You got the jester's curse," said Asadal.

"The what?"

"A jester. Someone who makes fun for the Emperor. Makes jokes. The magician laid on you the jester's curse."

Was that a common occurrence, Marius wondered? Were there hundreds of people walking around like him who had trouble walking normally and who couldn't put two words together without wearing a bewitched blade of grass?

"Is there a cure?"

"Cure?" Asadal smiled, not mocking Marius but in a sympathetic sort of way. "You can't cure magic. It's inside of you now. That's how magic works."

Marius cocked his head to the side. Agestah had said that Yavont of House Marcel might be able to help him find a cure.

"It's like this," said Asadal, again slipping into his thick accent. "Magic can only work on what's already there. See? To cure magic you got to cure what's inside." He patted Marius on the chest with an open hand. "Understand?"

Marius did not understand. He was also tired of looking stupid. So he kept his mouth shut.

"Still," said Asadal, "there's something about you and that curse I don't understand. We better ask Campri."

"Campri?"

"High Priest in Amok. Good man. We'll find him in Amok. Till then, we walk. Asadal will teach you the way of the Walker." He hustled Marius to his feet with the feeble-looking stick.

"Where are we going?" said Marius.

Asadal regarded him with his head stretched backwards, looking down his nose at the boy. "To Amok, like I said. Why? Does it matter?"

Marius thought about it. He had nowhere to go, nothing to do. He probably wouldn't even be alive if it weren't for the strangely dressed man.

"No."

Asadal smiled. "That is the first lesson of the Walker."

* * *

The thin stick flicked up from Asadal's legs to his chest in quick succession with every step. The man walked as though he were conducting a march, but instead of tambourines and fifes leading a wall of heavily armed soldiers, there was only Marius to follow.

They'd been walking together for the better part of the day. The sun was already in the teeth of the faraway hills. It cast a rosy glow over the cultivated fields visible through the trees lining the dirt road.

They had walked mainly in silence broken occasionally by Asadal's whistled assaults on music and good taste. Had no one ever told the man that he couldn't carry a tune or did he simply not care? Marius remembered a fellow slave who would hum to himself one low note, over and over. Only if it was a tune that had a recognizable rhythm, might one guess what the slave was humming. Maybe where Asadal had come from they had different ideas about what constituted music.

Marius watched the stick twitch up and down as though Asadal was fencing an invisible opponent. Finally, unable to stand the mystery any longer, he asked about it.

"Spiders," said Asadal. "Build their sticky webs across the road. Spiders are the bane of every Walker. Webs in your face, your beard, your hair. Then you feel the spider crawling over your skin whether it's there or not because sometimes it is. I once walked through a web only to discover, as I lay down to sleep, a spider as big as my fist atop my turban."

Marius found that his own skin had begun to itch at the thought of spiders hiding in his of clothing.

"In fact, that is a good lesson," said Asadal. "You take the stick and walk ahead of me."

Within five minutes of the new arrangement, Marius regretted having ever asked about the stick. After ten minutes, he became increasingly less diligent about waving it. Asadal said nothing.

Long, thin invisible strands caught him under the nose and on his lips. Marius waved the stick furiously, but it was too late. A spider web closed around his face as gentle and tight as a lover's grip. Marius reached up, batting it away, wiping off his face, his ears, and his hair.

Behind him, he could hear Asadal chuckling.

"The stick or the spider. That is the Walker's dilemma." The older man came alongside Marius. His long fingers reached for Marius's shoulder, removing a black and red-striped spider the size of a small coin.

Marius jumped to the side.

"Oh, it is not deadly." Asadal smiled revealing his unnaturally white teeth. He set the spider gently on the trunk of a nearby tree. "It's the ones with the red star on their backs you got to watch out for."

"A red star like an Astor?"

Marius thought he saw Asadal flinch.

"Why, you seen one?" asked the old Walker, eyeing Marius suspiciously.

"At House Cervix. With the wizard."

"It figures," said Asadal. "They go together like mold on fetid cheese. You got to watch out for Astors."

As the sun set, Marius waved the stick up and down, round and round, in front of him, unwilling to break another web with his face, especially not at dusk when it might be more difficult to discover a spider scuttling over his body.

"There," said Asadal. "That is what we have been looking for." He pointed to a low wall that ran along the lane. Near the wall was another road that led, Marius supposed, to a nearby farm. Marius could see nothing about the wall that distinguished it from hundreds of others they'd passed along the way.

"I don't—" he began.

Retrieving the stick from Marius's hands, Asadal pointed to a number of scratches near the base of the wall.

"Next lesson," said Asadal. "The signs of the Walkers. See here." He pointed to each scratch in succession.

"Is that writing?"

Asadal smiled. "In a way, though this language is older than Arovia or any speech left in this part of the world. It is picture writing, see? Old as the hills that surround us. This one," Asadal pointed to a bowl-shaped symbol, "says that we can sleep here in safety; while this one," he tapped on another glyph that looked like two sticks: one flat one sitting atop a stick that ran straight up and down in the shape of a "T."

"This one," said Asadal, "means we can work at the next farm in return for food."

"What does that last one mean?" asked Marius, indicating a third symbol that Asadal had skipped: an oblong circle bisected by a line.

"Eh, that one is—I'll explain when you're older," Asadal patted Marius on the back.

In Marius's experience, there was only one thing adults wouldn't tell you about till you were older. Couldn't Asadal see that he was nearly a man already? Somebody had to say something sometime.

Besides, it wasn't as though he hadn't learned about the way of the world from the domesticated animals and wild dogs that roamed the streets of Zeno.

"Asadal—" he began to object.

"Let's just say," Asadal adjusted the front of his shift uncomfortably, "you should not become too friendly with the farmer's daughter. The father might violently object, understand?"

"Oh."

"Yes." Asadal raised and lowered his eyebrows quickly in a way that made Marius smile. "Shall we bed down behind the wall? The sun will soon set."

Asadal took a little bag off his back. Marius hadn't even noticed it during their walk. It was as though the bag appeared out of nowhere. Perhaps it was where he'd been hiding the bread earlier. Its fabric matched the rough wool of his shift exactly.

Lying on the ground, Asadal placed his head atop the bag.

Marius placed his hands under his head and waited for the stars to come out.

"We need to get you a bindle," said Asadal, patting the small pouch under his head. "A bindle is where Walkers keep their valuables."

Marius thought if the man had anything really valuable he wouldn't be walking around in such scratchy looking cloth.

"Asadal, where do you come from?"

"Around the world. I've walked from free Caffir in the south, over the mighty mountains and into the southern provinces, all beholden to Arovia, all the way up the mainland of this empire and even to the barbaric north. I've seen the coast of Machoo in the far west, though a man such as you or me walks there at his peril. And now I am on the peninsula that is Arovia itself."

"But where are you from, I mean originally?"

Asadal sighed, "A Walker remembers every place he's been but home. That's the first rule of a Walker."

Marius shifted uncomfortably on the bare ground, feeling every pebble under his clothing.

Asadal continued, "I was born on a small island, far away in a vast sea, so vast not even I could walk across it." Asadal paused for a long moment. "Now get some sleep. We'll go to the farm tomorrow, see if they have any work for us Walkers. We'll earn our way down the road to Amok."

The idea of Asadal's sea, blue and stretching into the distance as far as the eye could see occupied Marius's imagination till sleep stole over him.

* * *

"Lift with the legs," Asadal said as he threw a bale of hay single-handedly atop the wagon.

"Don't bother trying to teach that hoosegow anything," said Limbago, the red-faced man atop the wagon who was stacking what Asadal and Marius tossed to him.

Marius and Asadal had moved from farm to farm for the past several weeks as they walked the long road that stretched toward Amok.

Marius was getting the hang of navigating the roads and of reading the marks on the signs. Though he still could not puzzle out the Arovian language, he'd become fluent in Walker writing.

Each official sign was decorated with the unofficial language, if not on the sign itself, then on the post or a wall nearby; or, if nothing else, by a stack of rocks carefully arranged. Marius felt fairly confident that he could make his way back to Zeno now and perhaps even back to the streets around the townhouse belonging to Cervix. Only, he had no desire to do so.

Occasionally, Marius saw a sign, one that Asadal wouldn't explain: a star with eyes sitting atop it. Asadal examined that mark carefully and would spend the rest of the day glancing over his shoulder.

Still, the old man was a pleasant enough companion. He'd found them some work on a farm to put a few coins in their pockets for the journey.

Farm labor was no harder than what Marius had been used to as a slave. True, house slaves had it better than field slaves and much better than the poor souls sent to the mines. Nevertheless, the life of a field hand wasn't bad.

Of course, if he got ill, the farmer had no duty to care for him. Thankfully, Marius was young and able-bodied. Yet he was still being outworked by the old Walker, Asadal.

The trick, Asadal told him, was not to wear yourself out with sustained effort but to pool your energy into a single burst, and then recover while the other fools worked themselves ragged. Asadal claimed he could work any man into the shade.

Marius didn't doubt it.

The only trouble with being a field hand was that, like being a slave, Marius didn't get to pick who he worked with.

Limbago up on the wagon was about as obnoxious a devil as Marius had ever met, besides Sivinius of course.

Limbago had inherited a shop which he'd drunk away. He now survived as did Marius and Asadal by the sweat of his brow. But having once been a prosperous free man, he never tired of lording it over the rest of the farm hands. Several workers had moved on to spite the man. The farmer, an old associate of Limbago's father, had kept him on out of a sense of obligation.

Having ascertained the truth of the matter, Asadal refused to leave, claiming that earning the good will of a man like the farmer was well worth the annoyance of a cretin like Limbago. He said that a Walker's life often depended on the kindness of old friends and former employers. Besides, Asadal claimed to have ways of taking care of men like Limbago, ways Marius had best learn if he wanted to survive as a Walker.

Survival, said Asadal, was the first rule of a Walker.

Asadal didn't blink when Marius reminded him of the other first rules he'd spoken about—of not minding too much where the road takes you or remembering home too fondly.

Asadal said there were many first rules and that he often forgot which was the firstmost.

"Hey Limbago," said Asadal as he threw a bale of hay atop the wagon. "Did you warn the boy about the snakes?"

Asadal winked.

Limbago took the hint. He played along with Asadal.

"Right, Asadal, big black snakes. Warn the boy to watch out as he picks up each bale. They like to hide in the cool shade between the sheaves."

"I haven't seen any—" said Marius.

Asadal cut him off. "Tie this bale for me, son, show me your skill." Asadal motioned to Marius.

While Marius struggled to pull the cut sheaves together tight enough to form a bale, Asadal knelt on the ground as though he were taking one of his frequent breaks. Marius saw that he had a short piece of rope in his hand and was rubbing it in the mud.

Marius shot him a questioning glance, which the old man ignored.

"All right, now that you got it tied, let me show you how to throw it proper."

"That's right, Asadal, show the pimpled whelp."

"You got to bend at the knees like this." Asadal bent low, gripping the bale around its base, under the first set of ropes that Marius had tied.

"Then you got to lift like this." He stood up quickly. The bale flew out of his hands toward the outstretched arms of Limbago. "And you got to mind the snakes!"

In the air with the bale was the thick, muddy cord, twitching in the wind just like a viper.

"Sheeeeooo—," Limbago never finished his exclamation. He fell backwards, teetering on the edge of the uppermost bale before landing, face-down, in the dirt and mud beside the wagon.

Marius began to laugh, but Asadal waved him off. "Later," he said. "Right now you got to get up on that wagon and finish this job so's we can get some dinner, understand?"

"Yeah, I understand," said Marius.

* * *

Later, he sat down beside the old man with a bowlful of gruel that had been handed to him by the farmer's pleasant wife. Not allowed inside the house, they sat outside against the wall.

"Ah, harvest," said Asadal. "My favorite times of year."

"It's not just once?"

"In the southernmost parts of Caffir and in the so-called barbarous north. But not here in lovely Arovia. In this weather, crops grow any time you plant them. All you got to do is wait." He took a bite of gruel. "Of course, they keep to a regular schedule. Three times a year. Don't you know this?"

Marius shrugged, "Not much need for a house slave to know anything beyond the end of his nose."

"Not all houses are like that," said Asadal. "Some teach their slaves, take them to church."

"Ha!" Marius coughed, choking on a bit of gruel. "Not House Cervix. Not exactly religious. Not bad masters, though, just—"

"And they wonder why their house withers on the vine."

The conversation had moved beyond Marius's ability to follow it, as often happened when the old man expounded on a bit of politics. Marius didn't have the head for it. But he was learning, slowly. Talking daily with Asadal was more education than he'd ever received. He was curious to know more.

"Have there always been s-s-slaves?"

Now it was Asadal's turn to smile at the naiveté of the youth. He never mocked Marius's ignorance. And he politely ignored the stutter that had been coming back slowly, no matter how many grass rings he made for the boy. This past time, when he'd given Marius a thick ring to replace the one that was fading, Asadal had worn a look of grave concern, though he'd said nothing.

Marius didn't ask what was bothering him. The first rule of a Walker, among many, was to appreciate life in the moment and not what may be. Bad as the horizon might look, appreciate the road under your feet.

"Suffice it to say," said Asadal, "there have always been slaves, though not always by that name. Take the farmer, is he free?"

"He hired us, makes his own schedule, and owns his own land."

"And is in turn owned by it and by those who buy his produce. And by the law and those who enforce it." Seeing what must have been a very confused look on Marius's face, Asadal continued. "Even the rich are owned by what they own. We call this the Chains of Gold. The children of House Cervix, were they free to do as they liked?"

Marius thought of the daughter to be wed, whether she liked it or not, to the fifth son of House Polonius. He shook his head, no.

"I know what you're thinking," said Asadal. "They have nice things. But they are controlled by those things. Possessions, houses, honor. All things that do not last in this world or in death."

Asadal continued, "The goal is to make yourself slave to a thing that truly matters. That is the first rule of the Walker."

Marius responded. "Aren't Walkers free? We go where we like. We owe nothing to no man. We own nothing that can bind us."

"Are you a Walker so soon?" said Asadal. "Ah, well, it's not as though we have a formal guild or application for membership, but if you truly want to be a Walker there are certain handshakes you must know." He paused, considering the original question. "No, dispossession is no more freeing than possession. We are all slaves to ourselves and our passions unless we are slaves to a thing greater than ourselves, understand?"

Marius shook his head, no, again.

"Oh, to be young again," said Asadal. "Let me put it in a way you might understand, and then let's drop the matter. You would, if you could, take any woman that would have you."

Marius began to object. Asadal overruled him with a wave.

"I was sixteen once."

"I can c-c-control myself," Marius scowled.

"Out of fear of what might happen to you if you did not? Like if you went into the kitchen and romanced the farmer's plump wife?"

"Asadal!"

"I joke, but only half-joke. What stops you?"

"Because it wouldn't be right!"

"Ah, then you enslave yourself to a higher power. Your idea of what is good."

"Doesn't everyone?"

"Sadly, no," said Asadal. "But here is the question that will keep you up many a night. How do you know that your conception of what is good is truly good?"

"Everybody knows right from wrong."

"Do they? I wish they did." Asadal leaned his head against the wall and promptly fell asleep.

Sleep when and where you can, he said, was another of the Walker's first rules. Marius suspected it had more to do with his advanced age.

The pause in the conversation gave Marius room to think about what Asadal had said. Didn't everyone know right from wrong? He thought of Flavorus who valued precision and order above all, even to the detriment of those who worked beneath him. His old majordomo was unbending in his pursuit of what he felt to be excellence. Flavorus was right in some ways, but the result was often wrong. And then there was Sivinius and Limbago, men whose idea of right and wrong revolved around their own best interests. There was the farmer they currently worked for, who seemed a good man. But was he any better than the townspeople outside the Cervix estate who'd laughed when their children threw rocks? There was the black-hearted mage who had cursed him and who apparently thought himself the definer of all right and wrong. And there was the priest whose idea of right and wrong came from outside himself entirely. Then there was Asadal and, of course, Marius himself, who had tried to set Sivinius on fire in order to get revenge on the man, no matter how badly he might be burned in the process. Of all the people he knew, maybe Agestah was the only one who was truly good.

Asadal's eyes were on him. The old man had awoken while Marius ruminated. The piercing gaze brought Marius out of his bleak reverie.

Asadal spoke quietly. "That is the secret of the magicians. They long to be the ones who define the good. The ones who control, manipulate, and enslave others. Blasphemy. That is why all magicians must die, understand?" The man put his head back against the wall, looking off at the sunset.

He'd get no argument from Marius, who'd just as soon see all wizards burn, especially the crooked-nosed mage who'd given him the jester's curse.

All of a sudden, Marius did see. He had a flash of insight and struggled to hold onto it as it rapidly faded. Asadal had once said that magic had to do with what was already inside you, and he now said that magic worked through manipulation. The magician said that Marius liked to make jokes and that he would make a joke of Marius. That must be how the curse worked, taking natural inclinations and twisting them.

He played nervously with the grass ring that Asadal made for him. The ring seemed a pitiful thing to pitch against the wizard's spell and his own self which were, together, working to destroy him.

\* \* \*

With harvest over, it felt good to be back on the road again. After a week on the road, they'd nearly run through the supplies the farmer's wife had insisted on sending them with. They hadn't objected

If the man had had a daughter his age or any interest in marrying her to a former slave, Marius might have been inclined to stick around.

As it was, they were once again walking the open roads of Arovia. Dusk was upon them, and they faced another night's sleep in the open. At least Marius had acquired a serviceable bindle made from a piece of scrap fabric given to him by the farmer's wife. He'd been horrified when Asadal had taken the bag from him and insisted on rubbing the new fabric in the dirt.

Don't look like you have anything worth stealing, said Asadal. And before he could complete the thought, Marius added for him, that's the first rule of the Walker.

Marius scanned the walls along the side of the road looking for a sign of a Walker to guide them to a safe resting place. Asadal's twig swished up and down.

On a post near the side of the road, Marius saw the mysterious sign, the one Asadal would never interpret: the symbol of a star drawn underneath a pair of roughly sketched eyes. The eyes were open. The star was darkened black. Other sketchings surrounded the star. Asadal's swarthy face became nearly as pale as Marius's.

In all their weeks together, Marius had learned a lot from the old man. In all that time, he'd never seen fear cross Asadal's face, even when Limbago threatened him with a pitchfork following the snake-tossing incident.

"Asadal?"

The old man recovered himself. "Marius, that is the sign of the Astors."

"A-astors?" He wondered why Asadal had never told him before.

Asadal continued, "The appointed guardians of Arovia."

"I k-know." Marius had heard stories about them: law-bringers who roamed Arovia exacting justice as they saw fit. Their authority was subject to the Emperor of Arovia, though few survived to make an appeal.

On the other hand, the roads of Arovia were amazingly clear of ruffians.

Marius wondered why Asadal had finally decided to tell him the meaning of the sign.

Asadal pointed with his stick. "Note the open eyes. They mean an Astor is on the alert, looking for something or someone. The blackened star means a bad Astor. Not many Astors are good. The lines underneath mean that this Astor has already killed Walkers. The two diagonal lines leaning against each other here," he hit them with the thin stick, "mean get away, fast."

"And the circle around the star?" said Marius.

"Means the Astor is not wearing a uniform. He could be anyone."

"How do we know how old the sign is? Maybe the Astor moved on?" said Marius.

Asadal gave him a hard look. His jaw clenched beneath the stubbled beard. "What did I tell you about the wind and the rain?"

"They w-w-wash marks away."

"How fresh is that mark?"

Marius examined it carefully. It did not seem to be as weathered as other marks he'd seen. The patina of weather stained the wall not over but underneath the mark.

"I d-d-don't—"

"A day, a week." Asadal pulled at his lower lip. He swatted the thin stick against his leg, thinking.

"Marius," he said quietly, so quiet that Marius had to strain to hear the man. "In the city of Amok is a priest. Campri is his name. He is the High Priest of Amok. If anything happens. If we get separated. You go on to Amok and find Campri, see?"

Marius nodded.

"Promise me. It's your curse. There's something about it— Campri might be able to help. I took you in, taught you everything I could about the Walkers. So, do this for me. Go to Amok, find Campri."

Asadal's speech was interrupted.

"What have we here, brother Walkers, I hoped someone might see that sign in time to survive like I have done."

A form stepped out of the trees near the road. In the gathering gloom of the coming night, it was difficult to make out who it might be. One thing was certain from the unmistakable curves. It was a woman.

"Well met, Walker," said Asadal.

Marius extended a hand, eager to practice the new handshakes. Asadal had initiated him into the way of the Walker by showing him certain secret clasps.

The thin stick barred his way. "Amok," Asadal whispered, "you promised."

"But that's a woman," Marius protested, "She can't—"

"Hold one moment, good friend," said Asadal aloud. "My young friend is sick in the head and distrustful of strangers. Let me calm him."

Turning close to Marius he acted as though he were comforting the young man. He added in a soothing voice, "Certain Astors have been looking for me, Marius." He put two fingers to the boy's mouth to prevent any outburst. "Not everyone is a Walker by choice, understand?" Asadal nodded slowly, waiting till Marius nodded with him. "Good. I'm sorry to do this to you, but it's for your own good. I don't think an Astor will bother with a fool."

He ripped the grass ring off of Marius's finger. Marius's eyes lit up with shock at being so betrayed.

"Amok. Campri," said Asadal. Then, hiking his shift between his legs and girding his loins with a loop of his colorful sash, Asadal ran. He ran faster than Marius had ever seen a man run, certainly an old man. It was one of his famous bursts of energy. He ran not down the road but into the deep bramble beside the road. Marius heard a splash as Asadal crossed a small stream.

Marius had forgotten the first rule of the Walker: when in doubt, run.

Before he could scramble, Marius found himself lying flat on his back in the middle of the road. The woman crouched with her knee on his chest and a wickedly curved knife at his throat. Beneath her beggar's robe, the woman was outfitted in black leather armor. A red star decorated her chest. Her brown hair was cut short and swept austerely away from her face. She was beautiful and terrifying.

"Who are you?" the woman asked. She let up enough on her knee for him to be able to breathe.

"Muh-muh-muh—" he began.

"Spit it out before I slit your throat. Who was that man?"

"I d-d-don't—"

"Ugh, you reek of magic," she said. Stepping off of him but still holding the point of the knife toward the soft part of his abdomen. "That was Asadal, wasn't it?"

"He-he-he—"

"Don't answer. I know what he's supposed to look like. I've been tracking him; got a good clue from a buddy of yours, name of Limbago."

She spat in the dirt. "So, Asadal leaves you here to die so he could escape. Typical."

"He w-w-wouldn't."

"Wouldn't he? He just did, idiot. Why do you think he was letting you travel with him in the first place? He changed things up. Thought I wouldn't be looking for two people traveling together. He's smart. I'll give him that much."

"He h-h-helped me."

"Did he?" The woman, who must be an Astor, looked at Marius with scorn. "Is that before or after he helped himself to your bindle?"

Marius reached around his back feeling for the pack. It was nowhere to be found.

"Did you ever leave the bindle with him? Or let him hold it?"

Marius nodded, thinking of how Asadal had rubbed the fabric in the mud to give it a rustic look.

"He put contraband in your bindle. If captured, you would have taken the blame." She shook her head. "It's just the sort of good friend Asadal is to stupid naïve new Walkers like you. Are you a runaway slave?" She took his silence for assent. "No matter. I don't deal in smalls."

Marius lay in the dirt as the sun set and the stars came out, reflecting weakly off of the sharp knife.

"Get up and walk. If you turn around, I kill you. I've got to track your best friend and can't very well do that with you behind me." She kicked Marius in his backside, prompting him roughly to his feet.

"If you see Asadal before I do, tell him Lespa says, 'Hi.' Now, run!" She waved the tip of her knife at him.

Dejected and defeated, Marius turned his back on the woman, all the while waiting to feel her blade between his ribs. He jogged, slowly, away.

"By the Lady what is wrong with you?" said the woman.

With the removal of the ring, Marius's curse had come back in full force. His legs ambled independent of one another, kicking up a heel here and turning and ankle there. His run looked like the ambulations of a bad puppeteer.

"That's some curse you have, fool," Lespa called after him.

Marius's fist shot up involuntarily with his thumb clasped between his fingers. The curse was going to get him killed for sure.

He heard a snort of laughter behind him. Apparently the curse knew its audience.

"Good one, fool. With that kind of pluck you might just make it in this world."

# Chapter 6

Marius was starving. Life as a slave had been comparatively easy. Life as a Walker had been pleasant enough, till Asadal's betrayal.

Marius now cursed the old man nearly as roundly as he did Sivinius and the magician.

Asadal had seemed kind, up until he'd left Marius to die at the hand of that crazy Astor, Lespa.

It had been nearly a month since Marius had run away from Lespa, all the while waiting for a killing blow that didn't come.

He'd wandered from village to village, looking for work, eating what he could scrounge.

Although Marius knew how to read the Walker's signs, they weren't much good to a fool who couldn't communicate without a terrible stutter and who couldn't trust his body to labor. Only the sign of the table with three loaves had been of any benefit to him—meaning that the farm or house might feed a beggar. So, a beggar he had become.

Marius remained too proud to steal, but his resolve wavered with his hunger and with every rock that hit him as the villagers drove him away.

He had last eaten four days ago. He'd been hungry then. Now, he was starving.

Marius huddled in the corner of the market in the town of Amok. He'd finally arrived in Amok. He'd come not out of obedience to Asadal but because of what Agestah had told him about Yavont, the majordomo House Marcel, and of the hoped-for cure.

And at any rate, Marius thought it might be easier for a beggar to survive in a city than in the rural countryside.

He didn't seek the high priest, Campri, and had no intention of doing so. Anyone allied with Asadal could go hang.

Marius wondered what sort of contraband Asadal was carrying and why Lespa had wanted Asadal so badly. In the end, it didn't matter. What mattered was how he had used Marius before deserting him, leaving him to find Amok on his own.

Now, Marius needed to find House Marcel. But before he could think of that, he needed to eat.

At midmorning, the market in Amok was as busy as it was ever likely to be. Located in an open square, the market was full of tables arranged to form irregular pathways large enough for carts to be pulled through. The carts were driven by the bulk purchasers, estates and inns whose slaves had come early to market.

Earlier that morning, each patron had been too well known, too recognizable for Marius to find the anonymity he needed for his purposes. He intended to steal what he needed to survive. He had read the Walker signs before entering the city of Amok. The city had a clean jail and the prisoners were fed and not tortured. It seemed as likely a place as any for Marius to start a life of crime.

The servants of smaller houses were shopping now as were those not fortunate enough to have servants: widows and unmarried maids. A few men also haggled over the vegetable stalls. Marius knew it was now or never. He pushed off the wall and tried to look casual and not so abnormally thin or desperate.

During the past month on the road, Marius had developed a comic limp. He teetered from heel to heel, making it difficult to blend in with the crowd. Marius tried to fit in, but his reddish tunic, now fraying at the edges, was not nearly clean enough to pass even a casual inspection.

It had seemed a minor insult of fate that Marius had been wearing his second-best tunic when he was kicked out of House Cervix; yet it was this simple fact, the cheapness of his cloth, that might draw attention and cause his death. Marius felt eyes on him as he passed the first vendor. He moved on to the next. Marius needed a distraction.

Young children walking through the market found Marius an object of curiosity. They pointed and laughed at the comical scarecrow—which he resembled, a thin man full of nothing but straw. His once large nose sat two sizes too big on his sunken cheeks, which, with his bulging eyes on either side of his gaunt face gave him the appearance of a spotted mackerel at the fishmonger's stall.

This too received comments from passersby, who hid their whispered remarks behind their hands but whose eyes traced the lines of his face and who always looked confused at the way his weak chin bled almost imperceptibly into his neck only to be over-shadowed by an enormous adam's apple.

Ignoring these glances, Marius focused on the task at hand—relieving some merchant of an over-abundance of food.

Finally, the distraction he needed materialized. An old man and a merchant broke into a heated exchange about the price of cabbage. Marius was standing beside a cart full of tomatoes. He snuck a few into his bony fingers and rued the fact that his pants held no pockets. He palmed the fruit as best he could, turning the back of his hands to hide his ill-gotten gain. Marius took a step backward. All eyes were on the fight. His head swam with hunger and the hope that he might actually succeed.

"Hey," someone called out. A young girl from a neighboring stall was looking at him. "Are you going to pay for that?"

Slowly, eyes turned from the argument to this new spectacle, which held more possibilities of entertainment. Everyone in the market inhaled at the same moment wanting to be the first to yell "thief."

Marius did not answer the girl. He ran, or tried to run. Marius was hampered by his weird, stumbling gait.

Shouts of "Thief!" rang out as the onlookers all cried in unison, each disappointed not to have shouted it preemptively and been proved right. Even the pair who had been arguing stopped to watch the scene of the tottering young man hurrying out of the market while being pursued and hemmed in by the other merchants and their assistants.

Some bystanders, who saw little risk in standing up against the feeble-looking young man, joined in the chase and later congratulated themselves on having such noble instincts.

Marius saw his escape cut off. He did not know the penalty for stealing or whether the merchants would leave enough of him alive to face the law.

He did the only thing that made sense. Marius stopped running and tried to eat the juiciest tomato. At least he wouldn't die on an empty belly.

He put the ripe fruit of the tomato toward his greedy, quivering lips. The fruit slipped in his hand. It squirted out of his grasp and rose into the air. He held up both hands to catch the precious fruit. The other tomatoes escaped. Each was like an eel in his grasp. He couldn't get a grip on any of the fruit. Each of the tomatoes touched his outstretched palm only to shoot into the air again. They cascaded up and down before his eyes.

He was juggling the fruit entirely by accident. He stumbled in an awkward, lazy semicircle following the movement of the fruit in the air. He only wanted to take a bite—one last bite—of fresh fruit before the merchants beat him to death.

Finally, out of desperation, Marius clasped both hands around the ripest tomato. It squirted out from between his palms, made a high arc in the air, and landed squarely on his upturned face, speared through the heart by his sharp nose. The other tomatoes likewise bounced off his face, smashing juice into his eyes. Marius looked down. The smashed tomato slid off his nose and into his hand. He wiped his eyes with his shirt and took a bite.

The crowd that had, seconds earlier, been poised for violence now watched in a baited silence.

Marius wanted to say something, to explain his extreme hunger and hardship. He opened his mouth to plead his case.

The curse took over.

"Tuh-tuh-tasty!" He stuttered uncontrollably.

The crowd burst into laughter. They waved their hands at him, begging him to stop. Some held their sides. Others wiped tears from their eyes.

"A fool," said one merchant.

"A juggler," said another.

The merchant from whom he had stolen was less amused. He demanded satisfaction for the tomatoes.

The crowd booed the merchant into silence and rained small coins down on Marius who quickly stooped to pick them up at the exact same time as the merchant. Their heads struck.

"Ooooh!" Marius groaned and clutched his wounded skull.

The crowd laughed all the harder and threw a few more coins. He clutched them tightly in his hands and looked up, smiling at the crowd. He didn't bother to pay the merchant, assuming the man had pocketed sufficient coins to cover the cost of a few paltry tomatoes.

Marius shuffled to a corner of the market where he hunkered down to count his coins. It wasn't much, but it seemed like a fortune to a former slave who'd never handled money.

He might've been promoted to majordomo, a position of responsibility, were it not for Sivinius.

Marius had thought more than once of how he might be revenged against Sivinius and the wizard, but he put these thoughts out of his mind. It was time to celebrate.

He ambled to a nearby inn. It was a seedy joint, one of the only places where he might be able to afford the food. Marius ordered a meal from the shared pot on the fire and a pint of watery ale. Taking a seat near a grimy window, Marius toasted himself before quaffing the beverage.

In moving the cup to his mouth, Marius spilled half of it down the front of his shirt. Since the night of his curse, he had developed a drinking problem. Only the grass ring bestowed upon him and then stolen by Asadal had provided any relief from the curse.

Marius had found that he could not drink from a cup without sticking his lips deliberately to the rim like a baby goat seeking its mother's teat. He now performed this stunt on the watery ale. A few patrons chuckled at the sight and raised a glass to him, thinking he must already be drunk.

Marius had difficulty eating as well. The bites didn't want to find his mouth. The first bite he took of the succulent, mysterious meat missed his mouth and hit him in the cheek. He had to physically slide it across his face in order to get the bite into his mouth. He must've looked like a distracted adult feeding a recalcitrant toddler.

Marius steadied his elbow on the table in front of his mouth. His hand moved unsteadily up and down. Marius followed the fork, moving his head like a chicken.

In this manner, he managed to feed himself, to the amusement of the entire establishment. They couldn't help but watch his antics. A few regulars who were already well into their cups despite the early hour patted him understandingly on the back. A sympathetic man slipped him a copper coin: enough to pay for the meal.

Marius stared at it in disbelief. Now that his belly was filling, thoughts came easier to mind. He had nearly starved to death, when, all along, he could have had his food paid for by the mere act of trying to eat.

During his travels, Marius had struggled to come to grips with what the wizard had done to him. He had been cursed. But as Asadal had intimated, it was no ordinary cursing. His flesh had not fallen off his bones nor had his skin turned ashen. Instead, whatever the wizard had done had made Marius incredibly clumsy—if that was the right word for it. Asadal had called it the jester's curse.

And yet, the more Marius thought about it, he realized that he was not always clumsy. It happened most often when other people were watching. His body behaved ridiculously, causing even casual observers to smile.

Marius tried to recall the wizard's exact words. Asadal, the Lady take him, had thought that was key to understanding the curse.

The white-robed, crooked-nosed man had threatened to make a funny joke on him. Ever since then, people had been laughing at him constantly.

But it wasn't till today that Marius saw the wizard's spell as anything other than a curse. Today, that curse had put food in his belly.

If things didn't work out with House Marcel, there might be another way out of his predicament, Marius realized. It would mean swallowing his pride, not that he had much left anyway. Survival was his only immediate concern; the first rule of the Walkers, right? Survival, and the thought of revenge on Sivinius and on the wizard who cursed him and on Asadal, too.

Vengeance, however, could only be had if he lived, and he could live only so long as he ate. Marius resolved to eat, whatever the cost to his pride.

He rose from the table to pay the barkeep. Of course, he tripped over his stool. Marius tucked his head and shoulders, and rolled, coming lightly to his feet. He wasn't surprised. Marius had begun to anticipate his body's betrayals.

Marius held a copper coin out to the barkeep, but as the man reached for it, the coin slid from between Marius's fingers. Marius caught it in the palm of his other hand. Opening that hand, however, he discovered the coin was no longer there. He felt it sliding down the front of his pants, down between his inner thighs. Marius squeezed his legs shut, trapping the there.

The barkeep was staring at the empty palm.

"That's a neat trick," said the man. "Show it to me and you won't pay for the food."

Marius wished he could. "I-I-I—" he stammered, trying to explain.

The man smiled and threw up his hands in mock surrender. "All right. Just pay for the ale then."

Marius still had the coins from the marketplace. He brought out a suitable one and held it toward the man. The coin collided with the bartender's meaty fingers. The small coin went flying. Marius reached with his free hand to grab it. He caught it behind the other man's ear, pulling the coin from behind the back of the man's head.

The man grinned.

"The old coin-in-the-ear-trick?" said the man. "My grandpaps used to do that one. Go on, keep it then." The barkeep shook his head and went back to his business, wiping down the bar's grimy counter with an even dirtier towel.

Marius couldn't think of what to say. "Thu-thu-thu," he began. Then, changing up, said, "Grateful to you." He said it in such a weird accent and fluctuation in tone that the man smiled all the more and waved him out of the bar as though dismissing a silly but sweet child.

"I've got paying customers. Get out, you rascal."

Marius shuffled backward so as not to dislodge the coin stuck between his thighs. The barkeep laughed and was joined by the patrons.

"He looks like an elf princess smuggling a cherry," said one.

"Like a bull holding in a prize dropping," called another.

"No," called the barkeep, "like a prince trying not to fart on his first date."

"Yeah, Prince Pratt," a man at the bar concurred, making a slippery raspberry sound.

"Prince Pratt! Prince Pratt!" The others joined in a chant that lasted till Marius got out the door, shutting it against their laughter.

Marius reached down the front of his pants, searching for the elusive copper coin. Now that no one was watching, he was sure to get ahold of it.

"Please don't do that in public."

Standing in front of him was a pair of beautiful eyes attached to an even prettier body clothed in the light blue tunic of a house slave. The color of the tunic complimented the girl's frizzy auburn hair, which marked her as a foreigner to the Arovian peninsula. So many slaves came from countries conquered by the empire.

Marius was grateful that she hadn't called the authorities about the pervert outside the inn.

He frantically removed his hand from his pants. When he looked up, the girl hadn't fled. She was looking at him with an eyebrow raised. She held a basket of groceries on an ample hip.

"I wondered how you would top the show at the market," she said. "I think the new act needs a little work."

Not trusting himself not to stutter, Marius gave her a look that he hoped conveyed the full extent of his apology at the situation.

"It's ok," she said. "My brother was a little bit like you. He—" She let the thought drift away as she blew the bangs out of her eyes.

"Anyway, see you around?" She waited for him to produce his name.

"Muh-muh-muh," he stuttered.

"Okay Muh-muh-muh." She cocked her head to one side. Her auburn hair bounced off her shoulder. "At least your name is original. Till to-mah-mah-mah-row then?"

She smiled.

Marius was shocked to discover that the smile included him, inviting him to smile back. He did.

Something inside him shivered, something near the broken wishbone the wizard had snagged. For once, he no longer cared how goofy he looked. She had seen him at his worst, with his hand down his pants, and she hadn't run away. It was more than he could have asked for.

She began to walk away.

"W-w-wait," he called after her. "Who are y-you?"

She looked over her shoulder and smiled. "I'm Irina of House Marcel."

He sidled after her, moving awkwardly holding his legs together to keep the coin from falling.

Irina of House Marcel. He marked the color of her light blue tunic in his mind.

"W-wait, I'm l-looking for House M-marcel."

She eyed him cautiously. "You are?"

He nodded comically. "I'm l-looking for Y-yavont."

The girl's face fell. "Yavont? But haven't you heard? Yavont is dead."

Marius's mouth gaped.

Irina touched him on the arm. "He died last year. I'm sorry."

Marius caught her arm, "An old s-slave of the house s-sent me. Agestah?"

Irina shook her head, "I've never heard of her."

Of course she hadn't, thought Marius, the girl seemed too young. Agestah had left House Marcel more than fifteen years ago, or so she'd said.

"She s-said I m-might find—" Marius paused. He didn't say "cure" as he didn't want to admit to the pretty girl that he'd been cursed. "She s-said I could find w-w-work?"

Irina frowned. The look was most unbecoming on her. "I don't think you want to work for House Marcel these days."

Marius's chest collapsed. He'd been holding out so much hope on finding Yavont and seeking a cure at House Marcel.

Irina, using the break in the conversation as an excuse to leave, turned and glided away.

The coin stuck in Marius's pants finally fell, rattling out the cuff of his and onto the stone-paved street. He watched Irina go before reaching for the copper coin.

So, Yavont was dead? Marius cursed his bad luck. So much for the cure he sought.

Still, as Irina turned the corner, Marius smiled. He had a feeling that he'd be staying in Amok for a while anyway. He felt he'd found something even better than a cure.

# Chapter 7

"Hey, Prince, catch!"

Marius put his hand up—a second too late, as always. An egg hit him in the face, cracking and sending yellow mucus down his nose. He sneezed.

Marius looked into his hands to discover a mixture of egg yolk and snot coating his fingers. He put on his stupidest grin.

The merchant who had baited him with the egg chuckled and tossed Marius a banana. It looked half rotten, true, but was a banana nonetheless. Rather than catch the exotic fruit normally, which he knew from experience would never happen, he leaned forward, clasping his hands behind his back. The banana landed in the small of his back and was trapped there. The merchant applauded the feat.

This stunt had been accomplished without the help of or interference from the curse. Marius discovered that the more he amused those around him, the more the curse left him alone.

If he tried playing it straight, the curse reacted in unexpected ways, though it could reliably be expected to include a blow to the groin. The curse found that gag particularly funny. To Marius's mind, a planned pratfall was better than a surprise blow to the crotch.

Marius hunkered down in the busy marketplace and pretended to eat the banana like a monkey he'd once seen at a traveling show in the crowded capitol city of Zeno. That had been a simpler, easier time—when he'd been a slave.

He ate like a fool and the curse left him alone, allowing him to gobble the sweet flesh of the banana in peace.

Similarly, over the previous weeks in Amok, Marius had learned to drink without spilling water down the front of his already filthy tunic. He stuck his tongue out of his mouth, lapping the air like a dog while pouring the liquid directly down the back of his throat. The method worked well for cool drinks, though he might have to develop a new technique to handle hot drinks when winter came to the peninsula. Not that winters were ever very harsh in Arovia.

The merchants around the square treated Marius like the village idiot's retarded brother.

Perhaps he was.

Marius had no way to communicate how much he understood of what was going on around him. Every time he tried to speak, his mouth racked with stutters. He felt stupid at not being able to compose a simple sentence. His cursed body wouldn't comply. So, he spoke seldom and listened much. And, though he was considered a mute-idiot, he showed such nimbleness at tricks like juggling and sleight of hand that the townsmen regarded him as perhaps less of an idiot and more like an idiot savant.

Marius quickly became a mascot to the merchants in market square. He slept in a vegetable stall in return for food paid out by the grateful merchant who no longer had to haul his produce from the market to his warehouse at night.

During the slow parts of the day, after the morning rush or before afternoon shoppers showed up, Marius would perform little juggling routines to entertain the merchants.

Inevitably one of the rotten fruit that he juggled would land on his head or slither down the back of his pants no matter how tightly he tied them. The curse just couldn't resist a good joke.

Slowly but surely, Marius improved his juggling skills. He didn't have a traditional, steady rhythm. Thanks to his curse, he probably never would. He developed instead a sense of comedic timing, allowing a fruit to drop nearly to the ground before kicking it up with his heel or catching a pear in the crook of his shoulder before popping it back into the routine.

As for the constant jeering and taunts, Marius patiently bore the humiliation. When it got too bad, or if a stranger threw a stone, one of the merchants usually stepped forward to defend him. He was, after all, their idiot.

They rewarded his antics with the occasional coin or a piece of produce only slightly rotten. One day, a cucumber vendor even gave him an old tunic—with pockets. Marius gratefully held his old, red tunic in reserve against an emergency, bundling it into a makeshift bindle to replace the one Asadal had stolen.

The coins he didn't dare keep in the bindle. He'd learned from his encounter with Asadal never to put all his possessions in one place. Marius found a loose brick in an alley near the church. It was as close as he ever wanted to get to High Priest Campri.

Marius had no need for religious rites and even less need to meet a person recommended by Asadal. Still, Marius hoped someone might think twice about stealing from a church, even if it was just a few coins in the wall.

As it had during his time as a slave, Marius's life in Amok quickly fell into a dull routine.

He had only vague plans for the future and for the vengeance he desired.

At sixteen, Marius considered himself capable of enduring nearly any circumstances, provided he never faced starvation as he had before coming to Amok.

The constant presence of Irina at the market might also have had something to do with his lack of plans.

He saw her nearly every day, wearing her light blue tunic as she bought produce for House Marcel.

Irina was the chief buyer for the kitchen of the greatest and richest house in the city.

Because House Marcel was rich, the rumors about them were that much nastier. It was said that they were hard masters, though Marius never saw a bruise on Irina or ever saw her without a smile. He knew that jealousy, like hunger, could cause tongues to wag.

Irina was kind to Marius, far kinder than anyone so beautiful had any reason to be. She brought him treats from the kitchen and sat by him while he ate, sharing all of the latest gossip from the town and from far away, as travelers came through Amok on their way to Zeno.

She reminded him of Agestah, his friend back in House Cervix, who also worked in the kitchen, though she ran the place.

What's more, Irina didn't seem to mind that Marius hardly spoke. In fact, in her presence the curse hardly operated at all. When Irina laughed, it was never at him. She disapproved of his making such a fool of himself in the market. But, of course, she couldn't know the truth—that his hijinks represented a defensive strategy to keep far worse things from happening.

That day, as Marius finished eating the banana, Irina arrived with news that concerned Marius. His ears perked up when she mentioned that Quintus Polonius of House Polonius had married the daughter of a lesser family, House Cervix. It was the talk of Amok that he'd taken the girl in exchange for a very handsome dowry, which included a country estate outside Zeno.

So, the merger that Sivinius anticipated had come to pass. As that whoreson had indicated, there would probably be a shuffling of the staff as slaves were given to the daughter to start her own home and as the husband brought in his own, trusted staff. Marius wondered where Sivinius had ended up, either in House Cervix or as part of the new branch of House Polonius. Cockroaches like Sivinius always survived.

No wonder he'd wanted to wait on the guests that night.

Then again, after that unfortunate event, Sivinius had probably acquired a choice position without difficulty, having some notoriety as the man set on fire by a clumsy, vindictive rival. His masters could show him off, telling the story for a year before people tired of it.

Wherever Sivinius ended up, Marius intended to find him one of these days. He'd have his revenge.

If Sivinius went with House Polonius, Flavorus, the old majordomo, would certainly not be sorry to see Sivinius leave. Marius tried not to feel bitter toward his old overseer. Aside from trying to beat Marius to death, Flavorus had been fair enough, though he never should have kept Sivinius in the house. He suffered the fate of anyone who kept a bad slave—same as smoke in the eyes or a bitter taste in the mouth as the old proverb went.

Marius hoped Agestah had come through the turmoil all right.

Sivinius had known that the promotion of House Cervix by marriage to House Polonius would be of benefit to the slaves. The Polonius estate in Zeno was massive compared to the humble home owned by Cervix. Also, to wear the purple tunic of a slave of House Polonius in Zeno was no small matter.

Marius lacked Sivinius's fascination with Zeno, seeing the disease and pestilence that festered inside the city like a rot in an otherwise healthy looking tooth.

The plague had taken both his parents when Marius was still a boy.

Instead of jealousy, Marius felt that he'd dodged a disease-ridden arrow. After all, when sickness struck, as it so often did in the city, rich families escaped to their country estates leaving the poor and the slaves to fend for themselves.

Still, being a slave in House Cervix was better than starving by the wayside or living as a beggar prince in the town of Amok.

Irina must have seen a look cross Marius's face as he processed this new information about his old house. She stopped the tale momentarily.

Opening his bindle, Marius pointed to the stained, red tunic.

"Not Polonius?" she asked.

He shook his head in the negative, his big nose batting the wind like a fan. Although the curse was abated somewhat in Irina's presence, he still didn't trust himself to speak without making a real fool out of himself. Irina had gone from being an audience for his curse's pranks to something more like a sister—albeit a sister that aroused the occasional incestuous thought. Marius found it comforting to be around Irina and didn't have to act comically in order to avoid a nasty surprise from the curse.

"House Cervix?" she asked.

He nodded.

Irina whistled. "Their estate is on the other side of Arovia."

Marius nodded again. He had walked a long way to get to Amok.

He'd been chased from town to town. A vagrant and a suspected runaway slave, he'd been treated little better than a mongrel dog—though he'd have been glad enough to have caught and eaten one of those scrawny little dogs. They were too canny and too fast.

Irina looked at the old uniform more closely, examining the sleeve and the cut of the cloth.

"You were a house slave?"

She looked at her own uniform. "They kicked you out, I bet. My house wouldn't take people like you either. My brother—" she let the statement fall flat. "I guess they got tired of you too?"

How could he explain to her that he hadn't always been like this, unable to put two words together, unable to walk without one knee bounding higher than the other? He'd been a slave like her. His mind was as quick as hers. He'd composed poems to her in his head many times over.

Instead, Marius raised his eyebrows and turned his lips wryly. He pointed to his head and made a circular motion, the universal sign for crazy.

"Something happened to you, didn't it?"

Marius bobbed his head up and down. If only she knew how Sivinius had set him up, put him right in the line of that black-hearted mage. Though, if he hadn't done so, Marius might never have met Irina. He wouldn't be sitting in the cool shade of the town square during a morning lull in foot traffic, conversing with an attractive, young, auburn-haired slave.

A fly crossed his nose. Marius moved to swat it and missed, delivering a tremendous slap to Irina's backside.

It was the curse. It had to be, but how to explain it? Marius looked around, only to see that they were being watched by a couple of merchants. The curse must have been aware of their prying eyes. One of them winked lasciviously at him.

"See if I ever bring you a snack again!" Irina stomped off in the direction of House Marcel. Her hips swayed back and forth with each step.

"Prince Pratt, you sly dog." One of the merchants walked over, clapping him on the back, his eyes fixed on Irina's retreating form. "Imagine being able to order that one to do whatever you wanted."

Though Marius knew what it was like to be a slave and what might happen, he hoped with all his heart, he almost knew to a certainty, that nothing like that had happened to Irina. She was too sweet, too nice. But if this merchant could think it, so could a member of House Marcel or one of their guests. Marius felt sick.

"Look, you've upset him. That's his girlfriend you're talking about," said the other merchant, good-naturedly enough.

"Our Prince thinks big," the first man scoffed.

"That's right. You'll never eat meat if you settle for the bone," responded the friend as they wandered, smiling, back to their stalls.

Marius wondered if Irina would ever forgive him.

He returned to the corner of the market that had almost become home to him. Setting his bindle on the paving stones, Marius practiced a few tosses with the bean-filled bags he'd recently constructed for his juggling routine.

Those merchants had assumed, as did Marius really, that he didn't have a chance with the pretty Irina and that he was as much a woman to her as her scullery friends.

He caught the beanbag on the back of his hand.

It wasn't necessarily such a bad thing, being seen as sexless. Marius knew what happened to male slaves who were perceived as threats to the honor of a family. He suspected certain merchants were also thinking that castrating the village idiot might not be such a bad idea as nothing good could come from a teenager with more genitals than sense.

In turn, Marius played the goofy, disinterested fool. If any of the merchants guessed the secret longings he harbored toward their daughters and even some of their wives, they'd have strung him up in an instant. The very thought caused his nethers to retract. It was a muscle he would never have thought to develop but that had proved useful given the maliciousness of his curse.

Still, Marius feared the time would soon come when he would have to remove himself from his comfortable existence in Market Square or face an awkward and painful operation.

Marius put a second beanbag into the air, catching each in turn with one hand.

Such were Marius's melancholy thoughts, mixed both with lust for Irina and alternatively thinking himself the most vile beast and a fool for sullying her honor on the altar of his base desires—she who occupied such a pedestal of female perfection. Never mind that he knew all too well the common fate of pretty slaves in powerful households. He couldn't imagine Irina without seeing in her all the virtue of the Lady of the Church herself, not that he believed in the Lady.

Marius remembered how the priest at House Cervix, after his prayer, had looked away from the crooked-nosed mage's powerful stare.

Could High Priest Campri have helped, really, Marius wondered? And would he, given how much the church despised all forms of magic? Lespa had said that Marius reeked of magic, having had a powerful curse laid upon him.

Marius tossed a third beanbag up with his free hand. He cycled them casually in a circle in front of his face, his eyes unfocused.

Marius had little learning. House Cervix didn't care for educated slaves. In other houses, Asadal had said, slaves were taught how to read and how to write, something Marius could not do.

Not believing in a soul, Marius readily would have given his in exchange for the ability to read and write or even for a hot, brothy meal.

Since all the slaves in House Cervix, save perhaps Flavorus (and Sivinius if his boasts were credible) were equally ignorant, Marius had never felt his lack of knowledge. Only when he'd traveled with Asadal and heard about the wide world had Marius discovered how little he truly knew about life.

Left on his own, Marius knew that he would have to learn in order to survive. Perhaps not how to read and write, at least not yet. He needed to learn how this new world worked if he was going to live in it. He resolved to listen and observe, absorbing all he could from the teeming marketplace of Amok before necessity forced him to move on.

Marius had already learned a little. He'd learned how to spot a dishonest vendor or a pick-pocket. He knew how to spot a false weight. He could anticipate when thieves were about to make a snatch-and-grab by the subtle change in crowd noise. He learned to recognize the signals used by the little thieves who worked in teams. One would cause a distraction while an accomplice pilfered a fruit basket. They never stole vegetables, which was unsurprising since none of the thieves were older than ten.

Given how harshly an Astor might punish a ring of thieves, Marius wasn't shocked that the only ones dumb enough to steal were kids too young to know any better. For instance, the children did not yet know that plant roots were much more nourishing than fruit in the long run, but what could one expect from the disaffected youth?

Marius only intervened if they stole from a vendor who had been kind to him. Not wanting to alert the thieves to his knowledge of their behavior, he would simply show up at an inopportune moment.

Marius returned his attention to his juggling, changing the pattern of the beanbags, moving hand under hand, alternating right and left, while catching and releasing the bags, pop-a-pop, pop-a-pop. The rhythm had a reassuring feel to it.

Not so with the thieves. Something about their activity scratched at the back of his mind, the place where self-preservation was most acute. It had taken him a week to identify the problem. They lacked organization. To someone who had grown up in a house run nearly as well as an army, Marius found the absence of leadership disturbing, almost offensive. These young thieves would surely be caught sooner or later, if not by the town watch, then, worse, by an Astor, those legendary enforcers like

Lespa, who roamed the land of Zeno with authority to kill any who broke the law.

So far, Marius had not seen any Astors in Amok. Nor had he been approached by anyone seeking to extort a share of his profits from begging. Such things were not unheard of among Walkers. That fact, combined with the disorganized young thieves who operated seemingly at will, led Marius to conclude that Amok lacked a larger crime base, a beggar king or similar leader. Not that such men or women lasted long once they came to the attention of an Astor like Lespa.

Or perhaps all the real thieves wore house colors and rode around in fancy carriages.

Watching the marketplace, Marius had learned to be wary. He'd learned not to let his guard down, though he didn't always succeed.

A hand snatched a beanbag out of the air. The other bags fell to the ground. Two men dressed in the light blue tunics of House Marcel stared at Marius. He hadn't seen them coming.

They both wore serious expressions. Marius wondered what Irina might've told them about the slap. He looked for a way to escape. The men had him trapped in the corner of the marketplace. Marius doubted any of the merchants would come to his aid this time, not against two well-built slaves from House Marcel.

Marius was on his own.

# Chapter 8

Putting up his hands as if to say, I don't want any trouble, Marius backed toward the wall. All he had to do was to slip free, grab his money out of the church wall, and get out of Amok.

Marius recognized one of the men. He had been hanging around the market in the past week without buying anything, strange behavior for a house slave indeed. The man had a nervous twitch, never quite looking Marius in the eyes.

The other man's face was unknown to Marius, though it did have a familiar look about it. His face was young and full of righteous self-import. He addressed Marius directly.

"Fool," the young man said, obviously meaning no disrespect by the term.

Water is wet, the sky is blue, and I'm a fool, thought Marius, what else should the man call me?

He was happy enough that the two men hadn't immediately set upon him, raining blows down on his head for what he'd accidentally done to Irina.

The young man straightened the front of his tunic officiously and continued, "The master of House Marcel has heard of your antics and wishes you to entertain his honored guests tomorrow night."

Marius wanted to object. He opened his mouth to speak, then closed it, knowing that any protest would be pointless with his broken speech. Besides, if he tried to deny his ability to entertain, the jester's curse would undoubtedly pick that moment to assert itself in an undeniable manner. And so, like the best kind of fool, Marius kept silent.

The young man said, "For this service, he will grant you a garment and two chickens."

The older slave nodded at the apparent fairness of this offer as though it were more than generous for the sort of simple distraction that Marius might provide the cultured guests.

The young man coughed before concluding. Marius could see that what followed wasn't on the official script. The young man looked uncomfortable.

"Fool, our master is generous with those who please him. But those who do not may find the famous hospitality of Amok somewhat less than advertised." He looked down his nose at Marius, unblinking, obviously hoping the fool would take the warning seriously.

Marius grinned like a buffoon and nodded. Up and down. Up and down. Very good, very good.

The man visibly relaxed. It was clear to Marius that the young man did not think the warning had really been understood. He'd relaxed, then, because he must have felt honor-bound to give it, even to the village idiot, which meant that the master of House Marcel was a piece of work. The rumors must, in fact, be true.

Though Marius had such little experience with decency that he didn't immediately recognize it in another human being, he decided that, for all his prickish behavior, the young slave was not such a bad person after all,

Wishing he could say the same of the other slave, Marius looked to him with the same goofy grin plastered on.

There was something about the darting eyes of the older, nervous slave that reminded Marius of someone; someone he couldn't place.

Plucking the beanbag out of the old man's hand, Marius tossed it into the air. He caught it, closing his hands over it. Gesturing for them to move closer, he opened his hands, revealing nothing. The bag had disappeared.

The young man smiled. His companion continued to look everywhere but at Marius. He gestured to the younger slave that they should leave. As they walked away in the same direction that Irina had gone, Marius caught several merchants staring out of the corners of their eyes. This little meeting would become local news by the end of the day.

He turned around, pretending to relieve himself on the wall. All eyes looked away in disgust. In reality, Marius was retrieving the beanbag from his pants, where it had landed, his curse shooting it down the front as always, delivering a vicious, glancing blow.

Even in that he was lucky. The curse had once caused a smaller beanbag to lodge in his throat, making him to run stomach-first into several neighboring carts before coughing it up, much to the delight of onlookers.

That was why he'd taken to practicing juggling. In just a few short weeks, his quick, sixteen-year-old reflexes had reacted marvelously, allowing him to master a few routines as well as some sleight of hand tricks that entertained the merchants.

Would these tricks also engage an audience of nobles? Marius was less sure about his ability to show them something new, and very sure of the warning he'd received. Marius had to perform tomorrow as though his life depended on it.

# Chapter 9

Marius awoke the next morning. The pile of mushy apples that he was lying on shifted beneath his weight, causing a landslide. His skull bounced off the bottom of the vegetable stall in which he slept. Marius preferred sleeping on leafy greens but, if tired enough, might sleep atop wicked-looking pineapples.

That night he had not slept well. His dreams had been disturbing.

Upon waking, his mind continued in the same vein, turning to the approaching evening. Again the thought ran though his mind: if he performed at House Marcel, his curse was going to have a field day.

He remembered the fateful banquet at House Cervix where his performance had consisted of nearly being beaten to death.

If he performed for House Marcel, Marius couldn't guarantee his own good behavior. He might drop a plate of fish on the matron's head. What would the vicious master of House Marcel say to that?

If he didn't go, he would become persona-non-grata in Amok. House Marcel might even have him killed.

Marius wondered if perhaps the time had come to move on. Having nearly starved to death on the road, he was in no hurry to leave the friendly faces he'd found in the square.

He could always leave before the party. That was at least two good meals away, nearly a lifetime in his estimation.

What was that rule of the Walkers, never refuse a meal? Or was it never think about the future? He could see how Asadal had a difficult time keeping all the first rules sorted.

Besides, he had to apologize to Irina. If he left now, without resolution, he knew their last meeting would haunt his dreams forever. Better to be dead than for Irina to think badly of him.

If the merchants knew why the two slaves from House Marcel had visited him, as they must, given how quickly gossip spread around the square, none of them had spoken of it. No one warned him away from the house. Maybe there was nothing to what the young man said after all. Maybe the man had been trying to scare him into complying.

Yet House Marcel had given Marius an ultimatum to appear before their master and his guests later that evening. Prince Pratt of Market Square had been ordered to make an appearance, though he intended to decline the invitation. His bindle was already packed—well, it was always packed since it contained so little. Marius planned to exit Amok as late as he possibly could without consequence. He would trust the Walker signs to point him toward a safe place to sleep.

Unfortunately for Marius, consequences were already set in motion.

Someone banged on the stall overhead.

Marius rolled out with his fists clenched, ready to fight, before he saw who had startled him. Irina had come to the market early, and she did not look happy.

Lying in the street, he saw Irina's delicate feet, smoothly clad in leather sandals. The arch of her naked foot was spectacularly intriguing.

Irina was looking at him expectantly, "Well?"

"I'm s-s-sorry!" It pained him to have to say it, betraying his ignorant stutter in front of her, but begging forgiveness was one thing he couldn't pantomime.

"Sorry about what?" she said.

Marius shrugged his shoulders and made a little swatting motion with his hand, reminding her of how he'd abused her bottom last time they met.

Irina pursed her lips, shaking her head. She'd never before looked at him as though he were an idiot. Today she did, and it nearly broke his heart.

"Who cares about that? What are you still doing here?"

Raising his hands toward his shoulders, Marius scrunched his eyebrows indicating that he had no idea what she was talking about.

"You aren't seriously going to perform tonight? Because my brother said—"

A wave of relief passed over Marius, so strong that it was almost a palpable thing. She wasn't mad about the liberty he'd accidentally taken with her backside yesterday. She wanted to talk about his upcoming visit to House Marcel. On that point, he could readily assure her.

He shook his head no while rippling his lips with a short blast, "Pfft," telling her that there was no way he was going to House Marcel that day or any other. Yet, her expression changed not to relief but fear.

"Then why didn't you flee when you had the chance?" she said. "Didn't my brother warn you?"

With a hand, he swept across market square as though he owned the place. This place had been good to him. Why should he run away?

"Are you really such a fool?" Irina stamped her foot in a way that made her auburn hair bounce.

She lowered her voice. "They've set a watch on you."

Marius turned his head back and forth.

"Stop looking."

In an arched doorway on the other side of the market, Marius saw the blue-robed, older slave who'd confronted him yesterday.

"Oh, I should have come back last night, should have warned you, but I was still too angry." Irina sighed. She put her face in her hands.

Marius wanted to throw his arms around her. He stood up, placing a long, bony hand on her shoulder. She shrugged it off.

"If you try to run, they will catch you. My master has spies all over the city. He knows everything. They will not let you leave Amok alive without performing, and even then, if you don't please my master—" She let the thought drop. "Ever since his wife died, my master has become—well, he's become a hard man, and without Yavont there's been no one to turn the brunt of his anger."

Marius tried to look nonchalant as though he faced such danger daily and paid it no mind. Inside, he was deeply disquieted. As a disgraced slave essentially on the run, his life was forfeit to whoever discovered his secret. Marius wondered how much the spies of House Marcel knew about him already.

He wondered if they knew about the brick in the alley behind the church that hid his savings.

There was only one thing to do. He needed to recover his coins and leave Amok.

Marius felt he could easily lose the old man in the city's alleys, curse or no curse. But first he had to get rid of Irina.

Yet, if he fled, they might think it was because Irina had warned him. She might be punished as a result. He had to do something to allay any suspicions. If she were angry at him yesterday, he hated to think how mad she'd be today.

"C-c-coin, Miss?" He circled around her, shambling in his silliest manner, his hands nearly dragging the ground.

Irina stared at him as though he'd just grown horns, and Marius thought he knew why.

He had never asked her for anything in all their visits together. He'd accepted the treats from the kitchen but had never made any request. He never acted the fool around her because he knew she didn't approve. There was something about Irina that made him want to be better.

A look of disgust marred her pretty features. Marius had betrayed their unspoken compact. The look said she was done with him, that she'd never be back to see him, never share a quiet moment alone with him. Maybe that was better for her, considering he was now being watched.

"Ugh," she grunted. "Why do I even bother with you?" She plunged a hand into her pocket and removed a small coin. She chucked it at his face. It hit him squarely in the eye.

The curse had never operated around her before. He could almost feel its glee at being released. Marius quickly sat down before the curse could make him do anything worse.

"To think I ever cared for you."

He grinned at her stupidly, though the look on his face did not match his heart. She had cared for him in a way, like a sister maybe. And he had certainly cared for her, though perhaps in a different way.

But the idea of them together had always been a fantasy. Marius had to break it off now in order to protect her. He noted the look of hurt in her eyes as her attitude shifted from pity to disdain.

You the virgin and I the prince, thought Marius without bitterness. It had been a pleasant time. But that was all. He now had more need of her coin than he would ever have of her company. Pleasant as she had been, their relationship had become a liability. She needed to get away from him as soon as possible, and he needed to retrieve his stash in the church wall.

There was one way to get rid of Irina, he knew. Marius did the previously unthinkable. He relaxed his iron control over his muscles and gave free reign to the curse.

It reacted immediately and with aplomb. Still sitting on the ground, Marius swung around till his back was toward her. Then he rolled backward. With his hands pressed into the small of his back, Marius pushed, allowing his legs to fall to the ground so that, doubled-over, his thighs framed his face.

Marius began beating a rhythm on his bottom. He made little spluttering noises with his tongue. "Oom-pa-pa-pthbbt! Oom-pa-pa-pthbbt!"

A sound of true shock passed Irina's lips. She stormed away.

So now you hate me too, thought Marius. Well, as they say, all roads eventually lead to Zeno. He had only provided her with a shortcut.

Marius uncurled and lay on the paving stones, resting on an elbow.

The poor girl would never know that he had just done her a favor. By playing the fool he had saved her from suspicion. Whatever Marius did next could only be blamed on him.

His instinct was to make for his cache before the rest of the city awoke and to break out of Amok during the morning rush through the city gates. He'd be out of Amok as fast as his gimpy gait would allow. It was a simple plan, one not even his curse could mess up, or so Marius hoped.

The only trouble was that he had to wait while the market filled with the early morning buyers, becoming busy enough to provide some distraction.

Purchasers from the major houses and inns walked full of purpose among the stalls. These transactions were prearranged based on years of habitual dealing. The merchants didn't bother calling out to this crowd, announcing their wares.

Attracting one of the big clients wasn't a matter of shouting your best price. It would mean catching a purchaser outside her house, plying her with gifts, perhaps a bribe or two to the kitchen staff. It also meant earning a lifelong enemy of the merchant whose client you stole. Marius had only seen one such transition during his time in the market, and the resulting fist fight had not been pretty. It was amazing what violence one could achieve with an oversized cumquat. A gourd had whipped through the air like the stoutest mace.

Marius waited till the crowd swelled and till the larger buyers began to drag carts into the streets laden with leafy greens, herbs, fruits, and an assortment of roots: red, white, and orange.

Marius had enjoyed quite a run in the market. True, besides Irina, he'd made few friends, but he had learned what he was capable of doing to survive and enough about life outside of slavery that he felt fairly positive about his chances of surviving on his own in the world. Even if he had to steal to eat, he had practically taken a master course by watching the young crooks prowling market square. He was reasonably certain that he'd never starve again. Also he'd learned enough of juggling and of pretend magic to put together a pretty good show, one that had caught the attention of the largest house in the city.

When a sizeable cart rolled past, Marius tucked his bindle under his arm and crouched behind the cart, putting the produce between him and the old slave that was spying on him. Based on the chartreuse livery of the slaves dragging the cart, it was bound for House Impus on the opposite end of the city, nowhere near the church. That was good. Before it turned out of the market, Marius ducked around a stall, doubling back. He kept low to the ground careful to avoid the notice of the merchants who were busy with the sort of talk associated with frequent customers passing the time.

He slipped into a narrow alley, he hoped without being detected. Marius suspected the old slave was following the big cart to House Impus. Meanwhile, Marius took a curving course to the church.

Normally when he traveled, he had no fear of interference. After all, who would steal from a poorly dressed fool? Nor did he worry about the curse acting up. With no one paying attention to him, the curse kept to itself. Marius ensured the curse stayed dormant by walking in a funny sort of half-trot on the tips of his toes, kicking a heel up every third or fourth step for no good reason at all. Or he loped goofily, bounding off walls and swinging around poles.

Now, however, knowing that eyes might be secretly on him, Marius worried that the curse would also be aware of the furtive audience and seek a way to make a show of even this simple escape from the city.

Another thought occurred to him. If the curse remained dormant, it might mean that no one was following him. The curse, then, might act like a sort of warning system that he was being watched.

In his right hand, he held the bindle. He let his left hand swing down near the front of his pants. The temptation to make Marius punch himself would be nearly irresistible to the curse if it sensed an audience. If anyone was watching the fool of market square, he would know about it.

Thankfully, the alleys were fairly clear. The types of people who frequented these alleys tended not to be early risers. The most Marius had to fear was getting a chamberpot emptied onto his head. He stepped gingerly around the detritus that had already hit the street, reminding him of his last day in House Cervix.

Marius reached the church. A few parishioners were leaving morning worship. They did so quietly and with their heads bowed. He waited till they were out of sight to slip down the alley beside the great building, hoping to find a quiet, unattended moment to remove the brick and pocket his savings.

Dropping the bindle, Marius pried at the edges of the loose brick with the tips of his fingers. Bits of mortar crumbled under his fingernails. The stone inched slowly out of the wall. Marius caught it in one hand. His other hand reached into the dark space of the church wall. His questing fingers found: nothing. His small pouch of coins was no longer there.

Marius banged his head against the wall wondering whether he'd truly been robbed or whether this was another trick of the spies of House Marcel. If someone had been watching him and knew he was to perform for the thrice-cursed master of that house, they must have known, like Irina, that his chances of surviving the performance were not great. Why not take his coins? He certainly wouldn't be needing them.

Marius realized too late that he should have split his meager coins among several hiding spots. As it was, his bindle now represented all his possessions. Wrapped up in a threadbare blanket attached to a stout stick were his spare tunic and other rare treasures, like a precious jar of sea salt acquired from a friendly merchant along with dried herbs given to him by another. Because the majority of his meals came from spoiled food, the herbs and salt helped to improve the taste.

Resetting the brick, sick at his stomach at the loss of his earnings, Marius decided to let the mystery of the stolen coins remain just that. He had to escape the city, surviving on his wits and what he had left in the bindle. As a Walker, he knew the rule: when in doubt, run.

Marius looked right and left, deciding to head behind the church rather than in front of it, where the wider street might afford potential spies a better chance of following him.

He found the alleyway suddenly blocked at both ends by a brace of men in light blue tunics. At the head of those nearest him was the young man from the day before. He twisted his hands together as though reluctant to share bad news.

"It seems you gave my companion the slip. We were assigned to watch this spot."

Were you also assigned to steal my coins, Marius wondered?

"I must insist that you come with us." The young man said it apologetically, but his companions looked as though they wouldn't mind pounding some sense into the village idiot's skull.

He considered whether the stick that supported his bindle might be used against the men in blue. More likely it would be taken out of his hands and used to beat him further. Marius kicked the bundle toward the wall, hoping to recover it should he come out of this alive.

The men started for him from both ends of the alley. Marius froze. But his curse did not. He hunkered down in the alley and soiled himself.

Marius sent a double barreled stream of waste into his pants. He was vaguely aware of what he was doing and was as surprised by it as the men seemed to be. That's when he dropped his pants, catching the muddy filth in his hands.

The men, their eyes growing wide, turned to retreat, their feet slipping on the cobble stones in a comical fashion almost worthy of the curse. To Marius, it all happened in slow motion. Like a spectator at an outdoor theater, Marius waited to see what the curse would do next. He expected to see feces flying at the retreating backs of his assailants. Instead, Marius covered himself in the foul stuff, smearing it up and down the tunic the merchant had given him, sticking solid bits into the pockets.

He then went as limp as a fish swimming in a sea of its own filth.

Inwardly Marius groaned. The tunic was ruined. The smell, much less the stains, would never come out.

On the other hand, perhaps there was a method to the curse's madness. The men would certainly not touch him in this condition.

He was wrong on that count.

The young man shook his head sympathetically at the sight of a grown man decorated in his own offal. He waved his larger companions over, giving them orders to pick Marius up.

Telling his body not to struggle, the curse made Marius all floppy, dead weight. It felt like the times he'd woken up in the middle of the night unable to move, still half-asleep.

The big goons carried him, a man under each leg and arm, down the quiet morning streets toward the gate that entered House Marcel.

So, thought Marius, he was going to work at House Marcel after all. Wouldn't Agestah be pleased?

# Chapter 10

Being unceremoniously dropped onto flag-stones by a bunch of goons who never wanted to touch his nasty body in the first place was a new, unpleasant experience. Almost as if they'd silently agreed, they jerked Marius up in unison to shoulder level before pushing him back toward the ground. He was able to protect his head at the expense of his ribs and knees.

The young slave stooped over beside Marius. "If it were up to me, I'd let you go. I had a brother like you, not right in the head." He paused. "My sister, Irina, wanted me to take it easy on you. I told Irina that I would try. But if you had not come, she would have been punished. Good-hearted as she is, she tried to warn you this morning and was seen. For her sake, I'm asking you not to run again."

Marius sat up, still covered in his own filth. He nodded his agreement.

So this was Irina's brother, or at least one of them. The other, apparently, was some kind of imbecile, same as Marius, or at least same as they thought Marius to be. Irina's kindness toward him made a lot more sense now. And the danger she was in because of it was something he couldn't allow.

Well, he was here now. Though he didn't see how he was going to entertain the guests of the most powerful house in the city covered in his own excrement. Maybe they wouldn't let him perform? Problem solved?

If they forced him to perform against his will, then he wouldn't feel the least bit sorry about the consequences should the curse kick in. After all, Irina and her brother were only on the hook for delivering Marius to the party. What happened once he got in the room was entirely on him and perhaps on everyone else should his curse get involved. He glanced down at the ruined clothes.

A month or two ago, Marius might have been concerned about his immediate future, but his near death experience at the grim hands of starvation had put some things into perspective. Also, he had the first rule of the Walkers to comfort him. Don't look at the horizon; be thankful for the road under your feet.

He was not going to die immediately. They needed him to perform. They couldn't beat him or break any limbs, at least not yet. Like one of their slaves, they had to feed him and take care of him.

Marius suddenly discovered that he needed to be taken care of very badly. Wants arose in his mind that he hadn't even known existed. For instance, he needed to try an unspoiled banana.

Under his new entitlement mentality, Marius began to see his ride across town as the procession of a famous performer borne in a gold gilt carriage on the backs of foreign slaves. Marius didn't even blink when Irina's brother led him into a beautifully tiled bathroom with a deep pool of refreshing water. He was a prince after all, Prince Pratt of Market Square, Amok.

"Wash off before you bathe."

The slave spoke as though Marius didn't know how to use a bathroom! True, he'd never actually used one. They were reserved for the members of the household or for the guests. He was a little surprised that they didn't take him out back and scrub him like a donkey. Maybe Irina's brother suspected that Marius might try to escape again and didn't fancy chasing a soap-covered, slippery, naked man down the busy streets of Amok. He'd probably weighed the wrath of the family at losing their entertainment to the wrath they might feel if they discovered that a vagabond had been let into their private bath.

"This is the guest bath. And my name is Ian," He started to extend a hand to grasp Marius's before thinking better of it. He looked Marius up and down, shaking his head. "Disrobe and we'll see to your clothing."

Seeing the suspicious look on Marius's face, he went on to explain, "Please do it. Otherwise, there are men outside who are anxious to give you a good dunking."

Marius turned around inside the bath. Colorful mosaic tiles lined the walls, floor, and ceiling, forming intricate patterns along with figures from myth and legend. If this was what the guests used, Marius wondered how nice the family bath must be. Agestah was right. House Marcel certainly was rich.

Everything he'd seen so far in House Marcel blew away the simple residence of House Cervix. This bathroom dwarfed the master bedroom in the Cervix family's city home. Of course, that was Zeno and this was merely Amok.

Still. Marius admired the two-story home of House Marcel. On the walk to the bath, he'd noticed that the garden in front of the house was immaculate. Scouting the exterior wall for avenues of escape, should the need present itself, Marius had been impressed that not a piece of paint was flecking off of the outer wall. No weeds poked up among the flagstones. The place shouted "money." He wished he'd had the chance to check the front wall for Walker's signs. What might they make of House Marcel?

His own presence inside the perfect courtyard went underappreciated. Anyone who came near, immediately fell back, offended by the dreadful wall of odor he presented. Noses were pinched and feet carried the slaves hurriedly in a different direction. Slaves disappeared from him as magically as Sivinius at that dropped chamberpot. Perhaps they feared being enlisted in cleaning up the trail of detritus left in his wake. Particles were falling off his clothing worse than off the bottom of a horse on parade. For once, Marius was glad he wasn't a slave—well, he still was a slave, technically—but not for House Marcel. He wouldn't have to clean up his own mess.

A small door on the bottom floor of the main house had been opened for him. And he'd found himself in this glorious bath where the floor was a circular mosaic pattern cut in a pattern resembling a peaceful, pastoral scene of greens that created the appearance of rolling hills, even though the floor was flat. There was even the occasional shepherd and sheep. On the ceiling was a bright yellow sun.

"Prince, if you'll please strip?" Ian broke into Marius's reverie.

Looking closely at the young man, Marius now saw the resemblance between Ian and his sister. They shared the same auburn hair, which clearly meant that at least one parent had not been born on the Arovian peninsula.

Marius was a native. Not that it did him much good. The blood flowing through his veins was as Arovian as any in the great houses. His nose was just as pointy and uncurved. Yet, he was a slave while others, just like him, separated only by an accident of birth, ruled the country and owned people like him.

"Are you quite ready, Prince?"

Wagging a long finger at the young man, Marius mockingly made a sign that Ian should cover his eyes, though he kept his finger well away from his face, considering it was still covered in filth.

Ian stared at Marius for a solid moment with a look of perfect incredulity. There was so little privacy in Arovian culture that the idea of a shy beggar must have seemed quite the farce. It also occurred to Marius that Ian might be reluctant to take his eyes off of his charge for other reasons. Perhaps he didn't trust Marius not to paint a brown mural on the walls of the guest bath.

In truth, Marius was not shy about his body. How could he be as a lowly house slave? He was concerned instead about what the curse might do before an audience. True, he hadn't felt the urge to act out since being alone in the young man's presence. Ian had something of his sister in him that way.

But Marius had learned the hard way to keep it simple around water. He'd taken a day trip to a stream that ran outside Amok, thinking to rinse the smell of the city and of his month long starvation off of his tunic. The curse had seen his dip in the stream as an opportunity to create a comedy of errors using slippery stones and a loose root on the shore to nearly drown him to death.

Looking around the bath, Marius saw plenty of opportunities for the curse to assert itself. He could step on the side of a wash-bucket causing it to bash his shin. He could slip on a bar of soap, knocking his head into the floor or wall. Worse, he could slip on the bath, catching the tall stoop between his legs.

To convince Ian of his sincerity, Marius did a little dance back and forth patting enthusiastically under his armpits, promising to bathe. He hated himself a little for having to put on such antics. But the more foolishly he acted, the more the curse let him be. So, he played the fool.

The part was gradually becoming second nature. It was getting difficult to say sometimes when his curse was acting and when it was just him being silly. Marius also found, despite some misgivings, a certain freedom in playing the fool. He hadn't had to do an honest day's work since arriving in Amok. Having once aspired to run House Cervix same as his old boss Flavorus, now he had no ambitions and no responsibilities either. His one regret was his dismal prospects for securing Irina's love.

Then again, his chances had never been that good. True, his parents had fallen in love and been allowed to marry and reproduce. Of course, the fruit of their union, namely Marius, benefited the house in the same way that a calf born to a prize cow would do.

Besides all this, there were two additional problems with a slave marriage to Irina. First, Marius didn't belong to House Marcel. And, second, Irina wasn't speaking to him.

Such were Marius's doleful thoughts, which followed in rapid succession. And it was all down to the curse. No girl would look twice at Prince Pratt.

As the curse had harmed him in his choice of companions, Marius was determined to keep the physical pain and further embarrassment to a minimum. So he insisted on not disrobing until Ian had turned to face the door.

Ian shoved a bucket of water toward Marius before complying.

Marius gladly shed the disgusting tunic. It was the first time he'd been naked in months.

His body had grown long and gaunt during his exile from House Marcel. He hardly recognized his own ribs. His stomach looked taut, like one of the wrestlers who entertained the masses in the Grand Arena in Zeno. His arm muscles looked huge from all the farm work he'd undertaken beside Asadal. He felt good.

Kicking his clothes in the direction of his reluctant captor, Marius reached into the bucket of water and began scrubbing. Thankfully, most of the worst bits had been on the clothes. Marius scrubbed the brown out from under his fingernails as best he could. He really wished that the curse hadn't wiped the muck through his hair, but of course it had. He didn't even want to think about what it would be like to turn his pockets inside out.

Marius spat out a trickle of water that had inadvertently entered his mouth, shuddering at the strange taste, and thought again of what he would do to that crooked-nosed magician or to Sivinius should he ever catch them alone and unawares. He turned to this, his second favorite daydream, since his favorite was denied him due to the close proximity of the object's brother.

Marius finished the first wash. He crossed the room, walking across the tiled, grassy fields toward the large bath.

He'd never had the luxury of a private bath. As a slave, he had never been allowed to attend a public bath in anything other than a supervisory capacity. Meanwhile, the public baths of Zeno couldn't compare to the opulence of the guest bathroom at House Marcel. The large bath, pool-like in size and enclosed in a knee-high wall, occupied the entire far side of the wall.

He slipped in, without incident, up to his armpits, his bottom resting on the floor of a bath that could have held ten more people comfortably. Marius resisted the urge to splash around.

The water was warm. He sank even further, up to his chin. Around the rim of the raised bath ran a little ledge that he could sit on while still remaining partially submerged.

If the church wanted him to believe in heaven, it should have used this bath as a recruitment tool. For a baptism in this bath once a week, Marius would have traded his soul and felt he'd gotten a bargain.

He moved onto the ledge, resting his back against the lip of the bath with his arms spread comfortably wide, floating on the surface of the pool. The bruises he'd earned from the rough handling at the hands of the slaves of House Marcel were soothed by the water.

The entirety of the huge room was warm and wet and thoroughly cozy. This was the way to live. Even if his life ended later as a result of his performance, Marius was glad to have had this moment.

In this bath, there was no use worrying about such petty things as continued existence. He had the urge to think deep, universal thoughts. He reviewed his juggling routines, looking for new ways to improve them. Marius mentally rehearsed the pick-pocket's sequence, bump and grab. He'd never used it himself, but it bore a strong resemblance to the sleight of hand tricks he'd developed for making coins disappear.

Marius's fingers had gotten quite nimble doing those tricks. He thought that he might be able to rob a rich man's pockets, should the opportunity present itself during the dinner performance. His old scruples against stealing had slowly been worn down by a life of poverty.

Sitting in this calming pool, he felt more than ever the unfairness of being born a slave rather than to a noble family. They hadn't earned their place any more than he merited slavery.

Why should he respect property that was merely a product of chance? Didn't men respect action? If so, then his action of stealing that which others had not worked to acquire made his claim over that property even better than theirs, because he'd at least had to achieve some skill, albeit at thieving. His claim had the better right.

These were the thoughts that the rich bath inspired, which is perhaps why the rich were so rapacious over the persons and property of the poor who they should be protecting. Of course, the thought never occurred to Marius that the bath had a spell put on it to aid the meditation of the bather, to align his interest subtly with that of House Marcel.

Marius only knew that he had to get clean in order to perform. He had to perform or else Irina, the girl that he loved, and her brother, and also Marius himself—slaves that they all were – might be executed by other slaves at the master's request.

His head swam as much as his body in that blue, clear bath.

Marius pinched his belly. There was such precious little fat on it now. A skinny man couldn't have many scruples, thought Marius. A skinny man had to do what the fat man said. Moral choices were best left to the fat and happy—who faced so few immediate challenges to their morality that they might deeply consider the subject at their leisure.

How unlike the skinny and the mean, the people of the street, who, having abandoned social morality for their own survival, were yet judged even more strictly for any perceived violations. Yes, judged to death and without the sort of trial or second chance that a fat citizen might get.

Marius appreciated the contemplative mood that the bath inspired. It was no wonder that the rich were so much smarter. Time to think was a luxury only the rich could afford.

He wondered what other luxuries he might be missing out on and might discover during the course of the day as he milked his visit to House Marcel for all it was worth. They would certainly have to feed him. And they could not put him back into those nasty clothes. The day was looking up.

He might have lost his small stash of savings, but a stolen silver fork would easily replace it. Were it not for the reputation of the master of House Marcel and the warnings from Irina and Ian, Marius would have been as happy and content as a newborn babe having all its needs and wants looked to. But part of his mind, a small part that he repeatedly tried to suppress, wondered what sort of torture lay in store for him. Another part of him, call it his pride, wondered how impressed the noble guests would be with the performance of Prince Pratt of Market Square.

If only he could've looked a few hours into the future, Marius might willingly have drowned himself right then.

# Chapter 11

He had to hand it to House Marcel. Their bath was excellent and their staff well trained. Ian had stood by for the better part of the morning while Marius luxuriated in the warm, healing waters of the spring-fed bath.

Those waters might have washed away his curse, he felt so good. He could have believed anything was possible after so nice a bath. But all good things must end, especially baths that leave one's fingers looking like albino raisins

Getting out of the bath, Marius checked again to make sure his attendant averted his eyes. He gamboled carefully out of the waters, waiting for the inevitable slip that never occurred.

Of course, even if Ian wasn't looking, he could still hear. Or didn't the curse think that sound was as funny as sight?

For whatever reason, Irina's brother also seemed immune to the workings of the curse. Perhaps it had something to do with that poor fool of a brother that had been mentioned in passing. Such close proximity to perpetual foolishness in someone they loved might have made it difficult for Irina or the brother to find humor in Marius's antics. In fact, his acting less of a fool had made Irina happy, and perhaps that was what the curse was after: making people smile. If such a person could exist in the world who found simple joy in the betterment of others instead of in their abuse, Marius was prepared to believe Irina might the one.

Ian held a clean towel behind his back.

Deciding to try his luck, Marius took the offered towel without any of the silly flourishes he might otherwise have made. He quickly ran the towel over his lean body before wrapping it around his waist.

Ian finally turned around.

"Th-th-thanks, Ih-Ih-Ih—" Marius struggled to pronounce the man's name. His stutter was still there, confirming that the curse had not actually been washed away, not even by that magical bath in the spectacularly appointed room.

Ian smiled. "Say it in one syllable: Een. That's how," he paused and the smile faded a bit, "that's how our brother used to do it."

"Een," Marius tried it tentatively, and to his surprise the trick worked. He wondered how many

other words he might compress down to one syllable and still make himself understood. If he spoke
them in an accent, people might think he was a foreigner instead of an idiot—were it not for his pronounced nose that would forever mark him as an
Arovian isthmuser.

Marius noted his companion's clouded features.
Ian had said, "That's how our brother used to do."
There was a story about their other brother that
neither Ian nor Irina was sharing.

Putting together the pieces, Irina had hinted that
House Marcel hadn't allowed their brother to be a
house slave like them. A master could make other
uses of an imbecile. They were usually incredibly
strong and might work in a stable. Or, he thought,
they might be sold to a mine. Or, worse, treated
like Marius and simply discarded from the house.

Maybe that was why Irina had taken such an interest in helping him. Perhaps he reminded her of
a brother that, like Marius, might be somewhere
out there on the road.

"Een?"

Ian's smile returned all the wider at the sound of
his name from Marius's lips. He took such obvious
pleasure in the simple recognition that Marius's
curse was stymied.

Marius wondered if that was another way to allay the curse. Instead of making a fool of himself,
he could find other ways to make people happy.
Yet, there were people in the world, like Sivinius,

who were only happy when other people looked more foolish than they did.

He could become a hermit, living out his days away from human contact, but he didn't like to think of the changes that even his meager lifestyle might undergo if he were forced to rely on his own devices to supply all his food and clothing.

Ian had shown him another option. If he ever found a place where the people would accept him for who he was and the simple pleasure that his company might bring, there he would remain forever.

House Marcel was not that place.

Marius decided to change the subject, "Een, d-did you know a s-slave named Agestah. She yuh-used to w-work here fif-fifteen years ago?"

The storm cloud passed over the young man's face once again. "No," he said. "I can't remember anyone by that name."

Ian was so obviously lying. Marius wondered why.

The door banged loudly inward. Marius checked the towel to make sure he was covered.

A thin, hunched man in a bright green tunic trimmed in flamboyant pink entered. His livery, if it were a uniform, was of no house that Marius knew.

"Old Huttle the Clothier," Ian announced.

The man had a pronounced lisp. "Here to dress the prince. Are you he?" Huttle eyed Marius up and down paying an inordinate amount of attention, Marius thought, on the down rather than the up. He paused a long moment, staring at the towel around Marius's waist.

"Right. I've got his measure."

"Just like that?" said Ian.

"I don't tell you how to milk cows."

"I don't milk cows."

"I wouldn't mind taking a more careful measure of his inseam," Huttle nodded toward Marius and smiled, "but I was taken to believe that we are on a tight schedule?"

"We need it today."

Old Huttle clucked his tongue. "Fit for a prince by today. What you must think of me?"

"I think you're the best."

The old man beamed at Ian. "Of course I am. I'll be back by the fourth bell."

"What am I supposed to dress him in now?" pleaded Ian.

The old man's lips engorged into a smile stretching ear to ear. "What's wrong with how nature made him?"

Old Huttle swept out of the room in a blur of green and pink.

Marius was glad the old man hadn't had time to take more exacting measures. When Marius saw the back of Old Huttle, he breathed a sigh of relief. Ian gave him a conspiratorial look.

"No matter what he says," said Ian, pointing back over his shoulder with a thumb, "you can't go out naked. I'll see to another set of clothing right away. Please wait here."

Marius was more than happy to do so. He'd never leave this room again given the chance.

"You won't cause any trouble, will you, Prince?"

Marius shook his head, no.

Ian gave a mocking bow and followed Huttle out of the small door in the wall.

Marius was alone in the room. Placing his hands firmly on his hips, now that no one was there to see him pose, Marius looked again around the room, taking in every detail. He might not ever get a chance to be in such another place. He might not even survive the night.

Even if he wanted to escape, he couldn't do so without risking Irina, and he definitely would not get very far naked.

Droplets of water spilled off the edges of his body. Marius put the thin towel he'd been given to work again. It looked more decorative than useful and brushed more water off his body than it absorbed. He was engaged in a little game of herding droplets of water off of his skin with the edge of the towel when another door opened in the wall opposite the original, small door. This one, too, presented a tiny opening.

Marius hadn't known there was another door. He wasn't expecting Ian back so soon. He returned the towel to its place around his waist.

A head of red, curly hair came through the door and with it a pair of green eyes, a delightfully curved smile, and not much else. That was all the adornment the woman wore. She was wrapped in a towel and, like Marius, might be every bit as naked underneath.

"I thought he would never leave," she said, twirling a strand of red hair in her fingers. "A prince comes to visit and nobody thought to tell me, Sybil of House Marcel?"

She was the sort of vision that kept sculptors up at night, feverishly pounding on their marble, knowing that whatever they made could never do her justice.

The woman was staring at Marius like he was a choice banana. She had the wrongest idea possible about who he really was. And he had no way of telling her that might not end with a painful death at the hands of the girl's father, the master of House Marcel.

# Chapter 12

I could see everything," said Sybil. "Everything," she repeated. "Isn't it decadent?" She pointed at a portion of the mosaic mural in the wall that depicted a leering half-man, half-fawn. On closer examination, Marius noticed that there were small holes where the eyes should have been and a big gaping hole at its mouth.

As Marius puzzled over the peep-holes in the mural, the redhead advanced toward him. Her face held all the perturbation of a woman who wasn't the sole object of male attention. As she moved, curves rippled up her body like a pond hit with a skipping stone.

Alarms rang in Marius's mind. Here was one of the daughters of House Marcel showing him much more of the female estate than he'd ever been meant to see.

He'd never had to deal with anything like this as a slave at House Cervix. Though a member of the family could do whatever they wanted with a slave, such advances were not always good for the slaves on the receiving end, especially those who received the attention of younger daughters. They often found themselves on a one way trip to the mines.

In Marius's case, he doubted they would take the trouble of shipping him all that way. The furthest he would go was as a corpse atop the refuse heap at the dung gate.

Marius took a careful step backwards, aware of all the ways his curse might avail itself of the awkward situation.

Sybil took a saucy step forward. "Of course, even decadence can be boring if you're a prince who's seen it all. But every once in a while a treat gets dropped in your lap."

Marius, who had never been the object of female attention, did not know how to manage this new development. Panic struggled against passion. He continued to retreat from her casual advance.

"What a spectacularly large nose you have, Prince." She examined him up and down nearly the same way that Old Huttle had. Marius didn't find himself any more comfortable under her gaze. "One can always tell royalty from their physical endowments."

The girl must have taken his mocking nickname, Prince Pratt, quite literally.

Marius saw the previous scene from her perspective behind the leering fawn with the open eyes and wide mouth.

She had seen Ian, a house slave, acting deferential toward Marius. Ian had even called him "prince" several times, as had Old Huttle. She must have taken all this as a confirmation of his rank, since he had indeed been acting as though he owned the place.

All this begged the question: why hadn't the curse taken advantage of the audience afforded by a pair of hidden eyes? Could it be that the curse was limited to Marius's own awareness of the audience?

Marius found himself circling the room, being backed up against the cold tile wall. Sybil stalked him.

He had been acting like he owned the place because he expected House Marcel would kill him later but had to care for him till his performance. The girl's father would certainly kill him at once if he became aware of the current scene.

Well, perhaps this was another advantage that Marius could take of House Marcel? He'd planned on stealing as much silver as his new outfit could hold and on eating as many choice foods as he could get out of the kitchen anyway. Why not this as well? He might as well enjoy himself. Wasn't that the first rule of a Walker?

At the thought of Walkers, Marius remembered the warning of the oblong circle bisected by a line. Don't get too close to the farmer's daughter.

He saw no possibility, with his limited speaking skills, of setting the record straight. And if he told her the truth, wouldn't her honor require his death?

That was all the justification that his sixteen-year-old body needed. And it wasn't as though the curse was going to let him out of a situation so rife with ironic and bawdy humor.

Seeing that she finally had him trapped, Sybil batted her eyes and bit her lower lip. "Oh, Prince, I'm sure that a country girl like me can't compete with the women of Zeno." She lifted her hands above her head and gathered her hair, letting it fall teasingly over her shoulders.

Marius pressed his back against the wall. The small tiles were cold on Marius's bottom. He clutched the towel around his waist.

She continued to stalk forward. Marius held up a hand to ward her off, some small part of him still conscious of self-preservation. She took it in her own, threading their fingers together. That was not what he'd intended.

"Oh, your hands are so rough and so strong. Do you hunt?"

She leaned in toward him, closing her eyes, extending a silky tongue through a pair of ripe, open lips.

Marius gave in to the moment. He closed his eyes, puckering his own mouth, ready for his first kiss.

He slipped. Marius jerked to the right. Sybil came face to face with the bathroom tile. She was kissing the leering fawn.

A look of mild shock contorted her otherwise beautiful face. Contact with the cold tile did nothing to squelch her ardor.

"Oh, your majesty! You tease me," In a quick movement, she reached for his towel.

Marius willed it to happen. But his curse had a will of its own.

Sybil clutched at air as Marius's hips swiveled to the side, avoiding her grasping hands.

She lunged and his hips jerked. She grabbed and the edge of the towel squirted free like a slithery fish.

Exasperation began to show. Sybil began using her nails. The curse continued to shift his hips around like an exotic belly dancer.

Sybil grabbed hard at the towel, scratching his waist with her sharp nails. Marius hopped back and forth.

"Why... won't... you... hold... still?" she said as she chased him around the room.

If she only knew how badly he wanted to do just that. The stupid curse wouldn't let him.

Finally, the back of his legs came into contact with the raised wall of the bath. There was nowhere else to go.

Sybil made one last lunge, launching both hands at the thin fabric that separated them. Marius slipped to his buttocks. She flew over him, her soft skin barely grazing his cheek. That was the cruelest joke of all—giving him that one moment of unrequited pleasure to remember forever.

Sybil tumbled face-first into the bath.

She remained under the water for what seemed an eternity.

What emerged no longer wore a loving, womanly face. Makeup bled down from the corners of her eyes. Her red hair was matted to her head. She came up spluttering, slapping the water.

"Am I not good enough for you?" Sybil spat out a mouthful of bath water. "Is House Marcel too low for a prince?"

She lumbered out of the water with none of the previous grace that had marked her movements. Her towel dripped all over the tiles. She stomped like a petulant child in a full-scale tantrum. The effect was not pretty.

Sybil gazed on him with scorn written across her face in spoiled makeup. "We shall see! We shall see!"

She was raving. Marius did not understand the exact nature of her threats. Were he a real prince he hardly would've cared. But all her shouting about using certain parts of his anatomy to choke earthworms not only hurt his pride but sounded like something that might be entirely within her power.

A stream of profanity flew from her lips so virulent that the foul-mouthed butcher at the market, had he heard it, might have renounced sin, sold his stall, and joined the church. She was on a roll, flinging invectives in Marius's direction when the door to the courtyard opened.

Ian stepped in.

Marius heard a squeak and saw a blur of red hair. The door framing the leering fawn slammed shut. He heard her wet feet slapping against the tiles as she ran away.

For his part, Ian merely raised an eyebrow. The look asked no question nor bore any malice or envy.

"You met Sybil?" He looked Marius over with a wry smile. "Though it seems you took less interest in her than most." He took Marius's tightly wrapped towel as a profession of virtue.

Handing Marius the light blue tunic of a house slave, he bade him put it on. "I'll have to loan you my spare clothing. Please no repeats from earlier."

Marius shook his long nose up and down agreeably. He was more than eager now to hide behind a shield of rough fabric, as though that could protect him from Sybil's revenge. The incident in the bathroom replayed itself over in his mind. He wanted to know the closeness of a woman.

Then again, had Ian discovered them, he certainly would have told Irina. And what would she have thought about his dalliance? Maybe she would have known that he didn't have the power to resist the advances of a member of the household. But probably she wouldn't have forgiven him.

Ian must have mistaken his glazed look. "You're lucky actually. The last slave that she took an interest in became something less than a man, if you know what I mean."

Marius shuddered. He could almost hear the protestations of his curse. Had it only known, it would have granted his every desire only to laugh about it later, even if it would deprive the curse of its favorite object of abuse. Apparently the curse didn't only work in physical humor; it had learned to appreciate irony as well.

"Hey, it's none of my business," said Ian. "Maybe you didn't like her. Maybe you'd rather I step out next time Old Huttle comes calling?"

No, Marius shook his head emphatically. Then his shoulders gave an involuntary shrug as if to say, "Well, maybe." That had been the curse talking.

Ian found the ambiguity funny. He smiled. "Irina said you were a laugh. I hope you entertain the guests at dinner tonight."

Me too, thought Marius. Me too. Then another thought occurred to him. Sybil would be at dinner. What would she think when she saw who the entertainment was?

Poor Ian. He'd probably thought the bath a safe place to stash Prince Pratt for a few moments unsupervised. Yet, in that short time, Marius had managed to make an enemy out of the daughter of the most powerful family in the city.

# Chapter 13

The sun had long since set. Marius stood outside the banquet hall waiting for the main course to be removed and the wine to be served. That would signal the start of his performance.

After the bath, Marius had lazed the day away on a bench in the courtyard while slaves rushed to and fro preparing for the night's festivities. Given time to reflect, Marius realized that even if he survived the pending performance, his life was forfeit if he stayed in Amok or anywhere within reach of Sybil.

Yet he was still alive for now, which was all that mattered. He'd been close to death before as a starving, wandering Walker.

The devil-may-care attitude of the fool of market square had slowly reasserted itself over the course of the day as Marius shrugged off his glum mood.

It certainly didn't hurt that the kitchen delivered a steady stream of small treats to his bench in the courtyard at Ian's orders. Plus, he'd seen a half-naked woman and even brushed against her smooth skin.

Marius's mind returned to the present. A slave rushed past him into the banquet hall carrying a full decanter of wine. Light from the walls and the overhead oil lamps played across the crystal jug sending a shower of small rainbows over the slave's clothing.

The beauty of House Marcel juxtaposed with the threat of violence was beyond Marius's reckoning. As for Sybil's very specific death threat, that was nothing when the perverse curse might at any moment decide to insult a homicidal maniac like the Astor Lespa just for laughs. Marius wondered how he'd survived as long as he had.

After the bath, he'd been left alone in the courtyard to watch the slaves rush around busily, which was entertainment enough for someone who, not a few months earlier, would have been doing the exact same thing.

Columns set at regular intervals a few feet inside the walled courtyard supported a small, tiled roof that provided a nice shade for Marius's bench. The surrounding wall created an enclosed garden space for the family almost as large as the market itself. House Marcel must indeed be wealthy and connected not just in Zeno, thought Marius. Sybil's red hair was not a product of the Arovian peninsula. Maybe House Marcel had ties to one of the southern provinces or beyond.

As a former, uneducated house slave, Marius lacked knowledge of the world outside his own house. But as to matters of running a small estate, he was something of an expert.

Watching the comings and goings of the slaves, Marius soon had a pretty good idea about the layout of the great house. Based on the slaves' movement, he even thought he could make a passable guess at which room on the upper floor belonged to Sybil. Though dangerous, her room still held a mystery that a sixteen-year-old couldn't ignore.

The kitchen and other common rooms, like the baths, were on the bottom floor, leaving the family rooms and guest rooms up above. A great central stairway in the middle of the house was a hub of activity, with slaves moving up it carrying great trays and returning empty handed. He thought it must lead to the dining hall.

He'd been right. Marius was even now standing at the top of those steps awaiting his entrance. He was very conscious of his position in relation to the rest of the estate.

Marius hoped that his knowledge of the house's layout might come in handy should he need to make a quick getaway after the performance.

They had closed the massive gates to the court-yard that emptied onto the street outside. Getting out of House Marcel was going to be difficult. Precautions taken to keep undesirables outside were also useful in keeping other people inside.

In his short time in the courtyard, Marius knew almost as much about the slaves of House Marcel as he knew about his own cohort at House Cervix. He recognized which slaves were in charge, which were incompetent, and which were having an affair and with whom, and which had recently broken up. All these details he'd absorbed as though they were second nature.

Even now, if he still wore Ian's light blue tunic instead of the crazy quilt of color that Huttle had sewn up for him, Marius could easily have picked up a tray and blended right in.

House Marcel was to Marius like an open and not very interesting book.

One thing did catch his eye, however. Many of the slaves showed signs of having recently been beaten.

Punishment was not unknown in House Cervix. Marius had been beaten for dropping the chamber-pot after all. Yet Flavorus was obsessed with productivity, and a wounded slave couldn't work as hard.

The signs of violence on House Marcel's own slaves did not bode well for Marius's safety. He nervously pulled at the hem of his new, colorful tunic.

Marius had told himself that this was the real reason he was so interested in watching the slaves—to look for things that might help him understand his situation or how he might escape.

Truth be told, he'd spent the whole day looking for Irina, hoping she'd come out of the kitchen or down the stairs. Yet he never saw her. The house was large, but it wasn't that large. She must have been avoiding him on purpose. And since he didn't have the run of the place, Irina had the advantage. She could go places he couldn't.

He only wanted to beg her forgiveness.

He was sure that she couldn't stay mad at him for his rude display in the market earlier, especially not in the ridiculous getup that Huttle had sewn him into.

She'd been angry that he hadn't fled the city at Ian's first warning. Yet, even though it had been foolish for him to remain, in retrospect Marius couldn't say for certain that he would have done anything differently.

He had feelings for Irina, feelings that he'd never expressed to her. He didn't want to leave Amok without telling her, without letting her know how he felt, even if she rejected him, as she undoubtedly would. Marius wanted to express his undying love for Irina, but he didn't know if she would take him seriously. The outfit certainly didn't help.

Old Huttle had created a piece of couture that fit like a glove, or more like an old glove patched many times over by a mad seamstress. It was a riot of quilted, colorful silk that could burn the eyes out of a blind man at thirty paces. The ensemble also fit much too snugly in the crotch, though even that was not without its benefits. Nothing he juggled could slip inadvertently down the impossibly tight waist of the pants, which again lacked pockets.

Thankfully, the red blouse and the multicolored vest contained many small pouches where he might secret the items of his profession and any spare silver.

Ian must have told Huttle that Marius was a street magician. Or perhaps Huttle had a thing for putting pockets on tops.

The legs of the pants and the shirt sleeves billowed out, leading Marius to think that Huttle had shown much greater attention to the fit at waist than to the rest of the outfit. No matter. The outfit was new, the fabric soft, and it smelled good.

He might embarrass himself in front of the important guests of House Marcel, but at least he'd do so in style. Hopefully the outfit would also prove a useful distraction while he pocketed pieces of silver from the tables before beating a hasty retreat out of the house and out of the city.

Waiting to take the center of the room, Marius wasn't struck with the same kind of stage fright that might affect a normal person before a big performance, especially one that his very life hung upon. Nor had he planned his performance the way a professional might. Marius had resigned himself to his fate.

Once the curse caught sight of the audience, it would grab hold and not let go until it had wrung every last laugh out of him, no matter how cruelly.

Ian bumped against Marius's shoulder as he prepared to enter the room to remove the dinner service.

"It's almost time. Do you need anything?" He glanced dubiously at Marius's empty hands. "Eggs to juggle or some tomatoes, Irina said the first time she saw you that—"

Ian never had a chance to finish his sentence. He gave Marius one last pleading glance. At a subtle signal from the recently appointed majordomo of House Marcel, all the slaves were required to clear the tables to make room for more wine and for desert.

It was obvious from Ian's last look that he didn't know what to expect from the night's performance. Then again, neither did Marius. Ian might be fearing a repeat of the scene that took place outside the church earlier. Marius certainly hoped not. With such tight pants, it wasn't clear how such a performance would come out.

Besides, he didn't think many of the fine persons assembled for the feast would be into that sort of humor, and he really hoped that his show would be good enough to keep himself and his friends out of further trouble.

Beyond that, he didn't really care what happened. He wasn't trying to get famous or rich. Neither was he seeking the instant infamy that the curse might generate.

Too soon and yet almost at the end of a forever-long wait, Marius heard himself being announced.

"Ladies and Gentlemen, few royals ever aspire to inspire and to entertain so well as this, our very own Prince Pratt of Market Square, whose majesty is dwarfed only by his sagacity."

A few diners chuckled at this bit of wit. Some in the room must have been familiar with the fool of a boy, Marius, who'd never spoken a wise word in his life or spoken at all if he could help it.

"Raise your glasses to your liege, your prince, Prince Pratt."

Marius heard knives and silverware banging on the table in anticipation of his entrance. He received a shove from behind, propelling him into the middle of the room.

The corridor, dark as it was, had poorly prepared him for the bright lights of the room. Marius put a hand to his face while his eyes adjusted. A few guests tittered about his mismatched outfit. Tables lined the walls leaving an open space in the middle. Marius occupied the center.

Upon removing his hand, Marius found the sight he'd been looking for and also dreading—the astonished and increasingly furious face of Sybil, seated beside her father, the head of House Marcel.

She began to rise.

Realizing that she might cause his immediate execution if she got going, Marius raised a hand in her direction. He grinned and waved. The audience looked to see who he was waiving at.

Sybil, flustered at the sudden attention and not knowing quite what to do, was momentarily frustrated in her attempt to have Marius killed. He took immediate advantage of the opportunity.

He continued the wave, wearing a goofy grin, and greeting each of the guests in turn with his best magisterial air. He took off his colorful, tasseled hat as though it were a crown and made a pantomime of bowing deeply. He hiccupped.

"That prince looks drunk," he heard one guest whisper.

At that exact moment, the curse leapt into action.

Marius became a spectator, just as curious as the audience to see what would happen next. Whatever it would be, Marius repeated a single phrase again and again in his mind, "Please not the crotch. Please not the crotch."

# Chapter 14

Marius staggered like a drunkard toward the nearest table. He drained an available glass of wine in one quaff before rolling the heavy cup over the back of his hand. It teetered on the verge of falling as he reeled around the room. With exaggerated movements, he returned it safely to the owner, patting the bottom of the glass lovingly. He got a few laughs.

Marius put a finger to his mouth and gave a drunken "Shhh!" That was enough to engage a few of the guests that were as drunk as Marius appeared.

Tripping over his feet, Marius walked over to the head table, waving over his shoulder as though inviting the audience along on a foolish, secretive quest.

He saw Sybil grab a knife. Marius stumbled into the table sending a loud clatter of dinner silver to the floor. Turning to the audience he gave a "shhh" again as if the audience had been the noisy one. Seeing his back, Sybil lunged with the knife.

The curse was ready. This time he didn't move away. Marius caught the knife hand, using her momentum to draw her into a very slobbery and ineffectual kiss that bounded off the side of her cheek. Knocking the knife out of her hand, Marius took both of her hands in his. Going down on one knee with Sybil lying over the table, he kissed both hands profusely. She had such nice rings. There was one with a ruby that must be worth a fortune, if he could only steal it. Unfortunately, the curse was in total control. Marius swept an arm back in a pantomime of universal love.

Marius was glad that Sybil had no magic. If she did, he'd have been burned alive from the look she gave him.

She ripped her hands free.

Marius fell to the floor, putting the back of his hand to his forehead, looking like the spurned lover.

Sybil threw a goblet at his head.

The audience was really getting into it. Marius could feel the curse feeding off their approval.

He caught the goblet and lapped at the spilled wine desperate as a thirsty dog.

Getting up unsteadily, Marius grabbed a carafe and refilled the goblet. He put a hand to the cup and then out to Sybil, as though the cup were a gift from his dearest love. She began to rise, till her father put a restraining hand on her shoulder, his lips curved upwards in a smile. That was a good sign, thought Marius. Had the father not approved of the fool's approach to his daughter, Marius might have been unceremoniously beaten to death. Perhaps the father knew about his daughter's reputation and hoped a subtle dig might put her in her place.

Marius oriented on the goblet. He tried to drink, but was suddenly too drunk to get the goblet to his lips. Oh, here was a joke Marius recognized.

He raised the goblet to his lips but missed at the last moment. Using both hands, he steadied the cup. He tried to raise it. But the glass was suddenly extremely heavy.

To the audience it looked as though the goblet were anchored in the air as fast as a tent stake. He appeared to pull on it again and again but was unable to move it. The glass was stuck.

He walked around it, one hand on the stem, pretending not to care, then pulled hard with both hands.

The glass didn't move.

Finally, feigning desperation, Marius got to his knees and approached the goblet at its level. As he went to drink, it shot up a foot in the air dragging his hands with it.

The audience had caught on to the act and was amused by his clever pantomime. Some got into it, yelling at him to try it again, that sobriety was for quitters.

Freeing a hand, Marius stood, acknowledging their remarks and urged them to be quiet so that he could concentrate on drinking. Turning a feverish look to the goblet, he gripped it firmly in both hands and pulled hard.

The goblet raced to his lips. The object of his desires seemed secured. Then it toppled suddenly in his hands. The audience gasped, thinking he would spill it down the front of his colorful tunic. Instead, the goblet tipped so hard that it spun, flipping all at once, so that not a drop spilled. He caught it on the bottom of the base and tried to sip.

The glass flipped again, away from him this time. Again, the momentum kept the liquid inside the crystal rim.

Marius repeated the movement, increasing in speed. Feigning desperation, he chased the flipping glass around the room. The audience felt he must drop the fast-spinning glass, that something had to happen, either his skill had to fail or gravity intervene. Till at last, something did happen.

Ducking quickly, Marius caught the spinning goblet atop his head and stood up.

The audience gasped. Marius waited to taste sweet wine as it poured down his head. But the glass did not overturn. Rather it was perched deliberately, right-side-up, on top of his head.

Drunkenly, Marius pretended to look for the glass, groping about with his hands outstretched.

"Your head, it's on your head!" The audience helped him.

Marius held a finger up as though to say, of course.

He reached for the glass. His head moved. He reached again but was unable to grasp it. As he went through the motions, much to the audience's delight, Marius caught sight of Sybil. She was sitting with her arms crossed, unamused by his antics, glowering at him, willing him to fail.

Never you fear, thought Marius. The curse will see to it that I fail spectacularly.

The audience shouted encouragement.

Finally, holding a finger aloft as though he'd come up with a brilliant idea worthy of royalty, Marius plucked a piece of fruit off a table and chucked it at his own head. It missed the glass. He caught it as it arced toward the floor. Marius grabbed another object off a table and threw it at the goblet, realizing as he did so that it was a knife. The audience gasped. The knife missed the glass too and came tumbling down. Marius closed his eyes as though he didn't want to see what happened next.

He caught the knife by the handle. The audience applauded. He tossed the fruit (it was an apple) at the glass and the knife at the same time. They crossed over his head. He threw them again. This time the apple connected with the goblet. He caught the goblet as it toppled, not spilling a drop of wine. He tossed it again into the air.

Marius was juggling the knife, the apple, and a goblet full of wine at the same time. His clumsy comic timing asserted itself, catching the glass at the last minute right before it hit the floor, kicking the apple back into the air, grabbing the knife accidentally by the blade and pretending to be stung by it while tossing it into another arc.

He bent low, chasing the items around the room as he moved them in a tight circle in front of his face, the knife always just missing his tragically large nose.

Somewhat detached from the action, since the curse was handling all the hard work, Marius let his eyes wander around the audience. He didn't dare try to reassert control over his body. If he did, he'd no doubt end up with a knife sticking through his hand. He would simply have to let the curse finish its act.

There was Sybil, still angry. But she had one eyebrow raised as though she appreciated his work. He noted a fat, friendly merchant from the market and gave him a wink and a nod. The merchant appreciated the acknowledgment and made sure that his companions had seen it as well.

The one face that he wanted to see was still absent. Marius was giving the performance of his life, and Irina wasn't there to see it. Of course, she'd been avoiding him all day. As a kitchen steward, it was unlikely that she'd be serving tables.

Maybe at House Cervix the footmen might put on the livery of a house slave and wait on guests, particularly if it was a large party. A house as rich as Marcel might think such a practice common, and maybe it was. Now that House Polonius controlled the country estate where Marius previously served, maybe things had changed with the influx of power and wealth.

Returning his mind to the action, Marius found that the knife, the apple, the goblet, and—much to his surprise—a wet potato and a small black cat had joined the routine, circling in front of his stooping face. He wondered momentarily how the cat had gotten involved in this mess. Maybe a guest had thrown it into the mix?

He looked around, trying to puzzle out the mystery. Looking back at him was another set of eyes that held a fiery, piercing stare. Not Sybil's. These eyes belonged to a man.

Marius recognized them as belonging to the old slave that had spied on him in the market. But what was a house slave doing sitting at one of the banqueting tables? The sight didn't make sense.

Then, Marius's stomach fell. As he watched, the old man's face changed, refining by degrees until it resembled the visage of a crooked-nosed magician. The man wore a long, lean smile. Marius dropped everything.

# Chapter 15

As the cat, the knife, the cup, the potato, and the apple shot toward the floor, his curse kicked back in. Scooping up the goblet and the knife just before impact, catching the apple and potato on the rebound, hooking the cat in the crook of his foot, they all went once more back into the air.

Marius struggled to regain mastery of his muscles. Revenge was so close, if he could only take control of the knife.

But the curse now acted as though it were playing to a very special audience. It exerted itself as Marius tossed the items higher and higher into the air. The audience gasped as the kitten soared within a whisker's breadth of the knife-blade before tumbling end-over-end back to Marius's hand only to be returned to the air.

The moment of culmination was fast approaching. Marius could feel it. The curse was building up to something big. He steeled himself against the inevitable pain, willing his nethers to shrink up into his abdomen.

He was standing in the middle of the room. The time for the finale had come.

The knife hit the apple, sinking into the core. He caught the knife by the handle and the goblet by its stem. The cat landed on top of his head, digging its tiny claws into his scalp. As he bent over to bow, the wet potato, oblivious to the impossible tightness of his pants, slipped down the back, lodging itself in his bottom.

Marius took a bite of the apple. The crowd roared. He shook the apple at the mischievous wine cup and raised it to his lips. Amazingly, the curse let him take a mighty swallow. The audience was overjoyed that the drunken fool finally achieved his goal.

He drained the glass. And he choked. Of course, it couldn't be that simple, not with the curse.

Marius couldn't breathe. He dropped the glass and clutched at his throat. The glass shattered on the floor. The audience thought it was a gag. It looked to be the curse's last laugh. The magician eyed him with a malevolent sneer. Marius backed up hard into a column. The cat skittered away.

He rammed his chest into the edge of a table. The people rolled with laughter. He did it again and again. His vision blurred.

Finally, with a last effort, Marius folded himself over the back of a chair.

Marius coughed. The object in his throat dislodged. He spat it into his hand. He was looking at a ring with an overlarge ruby. Sybil's ring. The curse must have stolen it after all.

Hardly aware of what he was doing, Marius strolled, like a debonair drunk, back to the head table and presented the ring to Sybil. She didn't dare slap it out of his hand as she no doubt wanted to do. The ring was too valuable. She took it in her palm, spit and all.

The audience loved it.

Sybil had already been intent on killing him. Marius was sure that his death was now at the very top of her agenda. She would have his head on a platter.

Perhaps not tonight though. Marius found himself taking a series of bows before a wildly enthusiastic crowd. His new-found popularity took him aback.

A voice at his side intoned, "Prince Pratt of Market Square, everyone. Now, please enjoy your desert course."

Marius was shuffled away by the majordomo into the corridor where he'd waited to begin his performance. Ian was patting him on the back. It was all over, well, except for the great escape that he'd be making right after he killed the wizard. Revenge was so close. Closer than Marius could ever know.

The wizard emerged from a dark shadow in the corridor, causing Marius to gasp in astonishment and fear. The wizard waved Ian away.

For his part, Ian gave the wizard such a look of loathing as he departed that it gave Marius courage. Marius swung the apple covered knife at the man's head. The wizard easily ducked the clumsy blow.

"You must be so tired after a performance like that," said the wizard. "Let me give you a little rest." He waved a hand.

Marius found that his limbs no longer responded to his commands.

"Magic is so clever isn't it? The way it takes a trait like tired and makes it exhausting, or a trait like silly and makes it ridiculous?" The wizard took Marius's face in his hand and turned it side to side, examining it like a widow-woman choosing a melon. His face was arrested in a knowing smile.

"You really are some of my best work," he said. "But you have disappointed me. You should be a complete and utter fool by now. Yet some of you is still in there." He tapped a long, crooked index finger, bent like his nose, on Marius's skull.

"The patterns are all there, within you, weaving together. But I felt my magic being resisted. I had to know why. I've been watching you." He gestured around the corridor. "And here we are."

"I thought," said the wizard, "I thought there was something special about you. But I was wrong. Wrong, wrong, wrong. I figured it out. It was her all along."

"Wh-wh-who?" Marius blurted, an icy cold pang went through his chest as though he knew the answer already.

"Your slave friend. She has a little magic in her." The wizard waggled the bent finger in Marius's face. "But I'll get it out of her. Yes, I'll get it and more from her tonight."

"I'll k-k-kill you!" said Marius.

"The stutter is a wonderful touch." The wizard smiled. "You won't stop me. Our dear Sybil has plans for you. Just as I have plans for your friend. It will be a very merry evening. She has been in my rooms all day waiting and waiting." He laced his fingers together, cracking his knuckles. "It's better for you really."

Marius glared at him.

"You may fight my curse, but it will consume you. You are a fly in my web. Without her help it will eat you inside. You may resist. It may take some time—a year—while you watch as you become more and more the fool. Oh, it's too much. Much too much." The wizard smirked as though this was the real performance for the evening. "Some of my best work."

"You b-b-b—"

The wizard interrupted, "Try saying it in a song. Yes, a silly song in a silly voice." He looked as though he had solved a great riddle. "Yes, try a limerick."

Marius clenched his jaw.

"No?" The wizard began to hum, "There once was a priest from Ephrapha... How does that go? Ah, pooh." He shrugged his shoulders, disappointed. His white robes rippled. "I am going to see your friend now. Good night." The wizard returned to the banquet hall, but he did not stop at his table. He was going to the guest rooms.

Marius had to do something.

As the invisible hands left him and Marius fell to the floor, he gave himself over to the curse. The wizard had said that the more he used it, the more it would take over. Asadal might have been worried about the same thing when the grass rings showed signs of not working.

But what choice did he have? Marius needed a distraction and the wizard's own curse was going to give it to him.

Marius rushed back into the banquet hall. The look on the majordomo's face was priceless. He ran into the middle of the room to stave Marius off, then, seeing he could not do so without causing a scene, announced:

"Ladies and Gentlemen, an encore from the one and only, Prince Pratt!"

The look on his officious face said he'd gladly hold Marius down while Sybil did her worst. Maybe the daughter had already given her new major-domo instructions concerning the fool.

Marius gave himself over to the curse whole-heartedly. In response, the curse flared up, sending his conscious mind into observation mode. As though he were detached from his own body, Marius watched the show. And this is what he saw:

# Chapter 16

The fool stood in the center of the bright room, his leggings and sleeves blossoming, his patchwork vest a riot of color. His low bow scraped the ground. His tasseled hat fell off his head. He bobbled it and, fumbling, dropped it to the ground where he proceeded to kick it around the room, seeming almost to have it in his grasp before his foot caught it again, sending it flying or having it get stuck like glue to the sole of his foot from which it would not come free for any amount of pulling.

It was an old routine, true, but still got a few laughs, especially since the wet potato was bulging like a docked dog's tail out of his extra-tight pants. The fool had neglected to remove it during the intermission. As though he finally realized his omission, he spread his legs wide and, bending at the knees, reached a hand deep into the back of his pants, searching for the tuber. The manifold grimaces playing across his face sent ripples through the audience. Finally, pulling the potato from his pants as though he'd discovered a gold coin on laundry day and looking furtively from side to side to make sure he was not observed, the fool popped the potato into his mouth and chewed. He ate it greedily, very pleased with the flavor, licking his fingers.

The fool wiped his hands together satisfied and took a step forward, slipping, of course, on his cap which was still on the ground. Finally, securing it in his hands, he shoved it down hard onto his head. The fool gave it a severe finger wag.

He pulled on it one last time for good measure, then, as if the cap had been a thinking cap that triggered the most wonderful idea, the fool held up his finger, opening his mouth in the universal sign of eureka. Then, pretending to forget, he put the finger to the side of his head and pulled his mouth in confusion.

"Tell, tell!" shouted someone in the audience.

The fool suddenly rediscovered his idea, raising his eyebrows brightly. Looking toward the man who'd shouted, the fool began reciting a limerick. He said, without stuttering a bit:

*I once saw a young man from Sallay*
*Assaulting a girl in an alley.*
*It's such fun being men,*
*The lad said with a grin.*
*Yet, he cried when I assaulted him.*

Every rhyme grew proportionally more ribald. The aristocrats loved it. They were deep in their cups now and were an easy audience to make merry.

One wag in the audience, the fat merchant with whom Marius had previously made eye contact, called for the fool to roast his companion, pointing to another well-known seafood vendor from the marketplace. The man looked exceedingly uncomfortable as the fool approached. The fool appeared to look the man up and down carefully before pronouncing judgment:

*This fishmonger's produce is super;*
*His fishes all seem to be newer.*
*But what will you find,*
*If you munch from his line?*
*That his catches all come from the sewer.*

The merchant's face glowed hot. The room roared. They slapped the fishmonger on the back and told him to relax. It was only a fool after all. And it wasn't the truth anyway. He didn't catch them in the sewer, as Marius knew from watching the market. He simply stored them there overnight.

Each guest cried out for the fool to skewer his neighbor. The women were not immune from his barbs and affected to protest when he took elaborate swipes at their virtue.

Before long, the fool ended up at the head table.

"A lark, a lark!" cried a boisterous guest.

"A fool!" cried another.

"A poem!" said a man who was too drunk to see the dark looks emanating from the host, the very head of House Marcel who controlled the entire town of Amok.

If the fool saw the warning in Marcel's eyes, he did not pay it any heed but bravely took in a deep breath and began:

> Our host for this marvelous feast
> Is heads above all men and beasts;
> Through the realm he is known
> As today he has shown
> For hospitable nobless oblige.

The leader of House Marcel smiled and nodded his head toward the fool. Aside from the man who had called for the poem, and who was probably ruined in Amok, the audience clapped politely. Though they might have been disappointed that the fool didn't bring old Marcel down a notch or two, they saw the sense in the act—what they didn't see was what made the fool sensible all of a sudden.

Turning to the daughter, the fool raised his eyebrows toward the host as though seeking permission to continue.

With a wave of the hand, permission was granted. That was what the fool had been counting on and why he'd gone so easy on old Marcel.

The audience grew silent. The fool cleared his throat and said:

*The daughter of noble Marcel*
*Is more talented than I can tell.*
*Why, not five hours thence*
*In the bath showed this prince*
*A performance without parallel!*

Sybil screamed. She threw a heavy plate at the fool's head. He ducked and spun in a circle, doing a jig, while the crowd, those too drunk to see danger brewing, roared at the joke. Others at the edge of the room began to exit quietly. They did not want to be remembered as having been in attendance that night.

Marcel was not laughing. He must have taken his daughter's rage as confirmation of the outlandish accusation. He knocked over the table and rushed at the fool with murder written across his face.

The fool continued his silly, triumphant dance, seemingly unaware of the man's approach. The man swung a fist at the fool who, surreptitiously ducking the blow, caused the man's arm to travel right through the sleeve of the fool's colorful vest.

Marcel swung his free arm at the fool's face. It too became enmeshed in the vest. After the briefest of struggles, Marcel ended up inside the fool's vest back to back with the man he was trying to kill.

Furious, Marcel reached for the fool but could not touch him. The fool popped his hips backward taking Marcel for a ride on his back around the room. He galloped like a horse, whinnying at the top of his lungs, "Neighhh! Neighhh!"

The majordomo looked as though he didn't know whether to interfere. The other slaves, used to their master's tirades, cowered in fear but were also a bit relieved that Marcel's fury might find a another target and were not a little amused at seeing the proud man so terribly abused by the fool.

Guards stood by with drawn swords.

Drunken guests who had less sense than the common slaves pointed and laughed.

The fool bounded off of several chairs in succession, hitting himself in the groin each time.

Finally, the vest ripped. The fool fell to the floor leaving Marcel standing, wearing scraps of the colorful cloth.

The fool's hat had been pulled tight over the old man's face. He groped blindly for the fool, but when he'd removed the hat from off his eyes, the fool was nowhere to be seen.

"Guards!" Marcel bellowed.

# Chapter 17

The corridors leading to the guest chambers were more elaborate than Marius had anticipated. Staircases wound up and down. What he had thought was a two story villa, from viewing the front of the house, extended far beyond the courtyard taking up whole city blocks.

The wizard had to be in one of the rooms with Irina. Doors lined the corridors. Oil lamps burned on walls painted a rich yellow and covered in tapestries. Marius remembered what Flavorus used to say: extravagant yet understated wealth signaled an old, established family.

Right now that staid household had been thrown into an uproar by Marius's performance. Noise of pursuit began to filter deeper into the house. Marius hoped the confusion as the slaves searched the house would be enough to distract the foul wizard from the object of his attention. But he was not counting on luck. Marius intended to search every room till he found Irina and put a knife in the wizard's throat.

Marius gripped the handle of the knife he'd stolen from the dinner hall for that very purpose. He hadn't succeeded in attacking the wizard in the hallway, but surprise was on his side this time. And with no one watching, the curse wouldn't get in his way.

A hand grabbed Marius by the shoulder, hauling him into a dark nook behind a tapestry. He spun on a heel, preparing to plunge the knife into his captor.

"Hold on!"

Ian stared at him wide eyed.

"What was all that about back there?" Ian thumbed over his shoulder. "That was—"

Stupid? Marius thought. Foolhardy?

"Amazing!" Ian finished. "You're a hero to us all."

That wouldn't stop the slaves who caught him from returning him to their master or beating him to death on orders, thought Marius. A group of guards swept by their hiding spot without pausing. Had Marius still been in the hallway he would have been captured.

Ian lowered his voice almost to a whisper, "But, seriously, why did you do that? You know Marcel's going to kill you now. And if he doesn't, Sybil will. And if she doesn't—"

Marius raised an eyebrow as if to say, get in line. He had people he wanted to kill too. First on his list was the wizard who even now was with Ian's sister.

"Eena?" said Marius.

"What?"

"Eena? Your s-s-sister?"

Ian shrugged, "I don't know. I haven't seen her all day."

So, she hadn't been hiding from him after all. The wizard really did have her. Marius put a knowing look on his face and nodded his head convincingly.

"The w-w-wizard has her."

Ian began to disagree, "No, that's—people leave her alone like that."

Of course they did, thought Marius. If what the wizard had said was true, Irina had a kind of magic that appealed to a person's better nature. Anyone with bad intentions toward her probably ended up remembering a mother that they hadn't seen or written nearly enough. It was a good trick for a pretty slave to have and gave serious reinforcement to the enormous pedestal that Marius already had Irina on.

Ian didn't know about his sister's magic. He might even have a similar talent. Ian also didn't know that the wizard wouldn't be affected by Irina's charm. From what Marius heard, acolytes of the magical arts didn't emerge from the White Tower with much of a conscience left to affect.

"Wizard. Which r-r-room?"

Doubt ran across Ian's face. That was a good start, thought Marius.

"It's right around the corner."

Footsteps echoed in the corridor, coming from the direction of the main hall. There was so little time. How could Marius explain the situation with his stutter?

Suddenly, he got the idea of using a rhyme as he had in the wondrously disastrous performance just moments earlier. Maybe a simple rhyme like he'd heard as a child would be sufficient to allay the curse.

Marius took a deep breath and quietly sang a verse to the old tune, the Brave Old Duke of Zeno:

*Oh, the wuh-wuh-wuh-wizard*
*Your sister he puh-plans*
*To ravage her body and soul*
*With his old wrinkled hands*
*And when he's done, she's done*
*Unless we can suh-soon*
*Convince the slaves ch-chasing me*
*I'm hiding in his room*

The content was so incongruous with the child-like nature of the rhyme that, except for botching a few words, the curse didn't even blink at the rest.

Awareness dawned on Ian's face followed by rage blending into impotence. The ravishing of slaves was a common occurrence and not against the law so long as the master consented. If the slave was family, you had to learn to look the other way—to pretend nothing had happened. But nothing like this ever had happened, not to Irina at least.

"What can we do? Marcel won't care if the wizard hurts her."

Had Ian not understood the plan, Marius wondered?

Sounds of pursuit were growing closer. Marius could hear doors banging open and rooms searched. It wouldn't be long before they thought to look behind the tapestry. It seemed like a place that many a slave might use to hide from an onerous duty.

Marius took Ian by the hand. "The w-w-wizard's room."

He sprinted into the hallway. No other slaves or guards were in sight. Ian, getting the idea, took the lead, running through the corridor, turning the corner, he began counting doors.

"It's this one."

Marius put an ear to the door. He didn't hear any noises coming from within, but maybe the wizard had ways of shielding the cries of his captives or maybe he had seized up her limbs as he'd done to Marius outside the banquet hall making it impossible for Irina to resist.

He banged impetuously on the door.

Ian pulled him back.

Marius looked around the corridor. He spied another tapestry hanging beside the door.

"C-c-all the guards. Tell them, in th-th-there. Save Eena."

Ian nodded. Marius ducked behind the tapestry, holding his knife at the ready.

"Hey!" Ian shouted. "Over here, quick!"

Marius heard a rushing of feet and the dull muttering associated with a group of people too big for an enclosed space.

"What did you say?" the man who must be the leader of the gang spoke.

"I saw the fool in a red shirt slip behind this door."

The door handle rattled. "It's locked."

"He must have locked it."

"Whose room is it?"

"How should I know?"

"Aren't you a house slave? Don't you know who's staying in each room?"

"Aren't you a door guard? Don't you know every face that passes?" said Ian. "Hey, is there a reward or something?"

"Nothing that you'll ever see."

There was a furious pounding on the door, the vibrations of which crept through the wall, rattling Marius's head.

The guard knocked again. "Open up. We have orders to search the house."

The door opened. This was the most dangerous part, thought Marius. When the guards saw whose room it was, they would probably begin apologizing abjectly and hoping not to be turned into a toad or worse.

Instead, the guard said in a rough voice, "Please step aside. And put on some more clothing for the Lady's sake."

The wizard wasn't wearing his white robes. They hadn't recognized him. It was a mistake Marius was sure they'd regret.

"What is this all about?" cried a furious voice. Through the crack between the tapestry and the wall, Marius saw men trooping into the room.

"This is an outrage," said the wizard, "Wait till I tell Marcel."

"It was Marcel who ordered it," said the guard.

"Did he now?" There was a malevolent tone in the wizard's voice. He seemed to assume that the search was a personal betrayal by the head of House Marcel.

Well, if the wizard and Marcel came to blows, that could only help Marius, since both wished him evil.

"Irina, there you are!"

Marius heard Ian feigning a reproachful voice inside the room.

"I've been looking for you. We've all been ordered to search for the fool who escaped after his last performance. I thought I saw him come in here."

"The fool?" asked the wizard.

"That fool," said the guard, "got him a death wish. He insulted Marcel and the daughter. Going to be split limb from limb by a pair of wild boars before they eat his belly out."

A little chuckle arose from the wizard. "That's really too bad."

"The room is empty," another disembodied voice reported. "No sign of him in here."

Marius could see very little from behind the tapestry.

"Sorry to disturb you," said the door guard.

The wizard now stepped into the hallway, dressed only in a pair of loose, baggy pants.

Ian led Irina out of the door. Thankfully, she was fully dressed, though her hair was disheveled and her eyes looked as though she'd been crying all day.

"Wait," called the wizard. "The female slave, leave her...urk—" he stopped talking.

Marius had the tip of his knife poking into the man's bare lower back.

"Come on." said the guard to the others. They began trooping away.

The wizard whispered over his shoulder. "Well played, fool. But if you kill me now, they'll discover you instantly."

Marius pushed the tip of the dagger even more sharply into the layer of fat extending from the man's belly around his lower back Unfortunately, the man was right.

"Hey!" Ian's voice carried down the hallway. "There he goes down the stairs!"

Perhaps sensing Marius's resolution waiver, the wizard called after the guards, "Wait. I'm coming with you."

Over his shoulder he added. "We will meet again, fool. Pity I never got started on your friend. But her time will come soon enough."

He walked calmly away. Marius crouched behind the tapestry waiting for the wizard to turn around and expose him. Marius was ready to rush him the second he began incanting a spell. He wouldn't be trapped again by the man's magic—not if he could help it.

But the wizard did not turn.

When he'd cleared the corner, Marius sprinted in the other direction before the wizard could alert the guards to his presence. He'd done as much as he could for Irina. Ian would have to do the rest. Escape was the only thing now on Marius's mind.

# Chapter 18

Marius raced down corridors. The map that he'd built all day in his mind was no good at all. The town house was more expansive than he'd ever imagined. What he wouldn't give for a few Walker's signs on the walls.

He reasoned that, if he could only come to the end of the hall, he might find a window that let out onto the street. That he was still on the second floor did not give him much pause. He hoped there might be a pipe to shimmy down. Even a jump, while it might twist an ankle, would hurt less than what Marcel and his daughter had in mind.

Finally he saw the end of the hallway approaching. He also heard footsteps coming toward him from deeper inside the house. The diversion Ian had created must have finally run its course. They were looking for him again in earnest and, having searched all the wrong places, were narrowing it down. It was no good playing hide and seek in someone else's house.

Tucking the knife carefully into his shirt, Marius tried the nearest door. It was locked. Bolted from the inside. Some of the guests must have suspected Marcel would be on the rampage and had taken precautions. Had it been Marius in the room, he would have shoved every piece of furniture against the door just to be safe.

The next room looked good for a window over the street. Marius tried the handle as well.

"Open up," he said. "We're looking for a thief."

"I will open for Marcel himself and no one else," came a deep voice from behind the door.

The man was bluffing, Marius thought, but so was he.

"Fine, I'm going to get him now." Let the man sweat for the rest of the night.

All he needed was a window, a chance to scurry down into the street and to disappear from Amok and maybe even the whole country. It wasn't as though he'd be safe anywhere he went. Not even a big city like Zeno might hide someone who House Marcel wanted found. And it wasn't as though Marius was inconspicuous. He stood out in a crowd like a pimple on a bride.

He tried the final door. If it didn't work, he was going to be in a lot of trouble. Footsteps echoed down the corridor coming ever closer.

Marius tried the handle. It turned. The door was not locked. He pushed. Neither was it bolted. Perhaps the room at the end was empty or its owner had yet to return from the banquet. It was the break he needed. Not even his curse could mess up this piece of luck.

Marius opened and closed the door quietly. Throwing the lock behind him, he placed a large bar across the door.

The room was dark. He didn't bother lighting a candle. Sufficient light entered the room through a window, too small to crawl through. Marius guessed it was another protective measure for the guest's security.

It was strange to think that one would put such a sturdy bolt on a guest room. But the politics of the realm made guests a little wary of assassination. The extra security created the appearance of safety and of considerate hospitality.

Marius shoved furniture in front of the door. The heavy chest of drawers went up against the door nicely. He was in the process of moving the bed, scratching the surface of the tiled floor, when a voice called out.

"Hello? Is someone there?"

A small door stood open on the far wall. He heard the sound of a tinder box and saw a small light that could only come from a candle peeking through the crack of the door.

Marius went to investigate. He hoped whoever belonged to the voice, which sounded frail and old, wouldn't put up a fight.

Looking into the room, Marius saw a man seated on a low bench with a set of dark blue robes pulled up around his waist. The robe immediately signaled that this was a man of the church, a priest.

"Your door was unlocked," said Marius.

"I didn't think anyone would, ah, burgle a priest. I haven't much to steal and the penalty is eternal." The white haired man examined Marius through the door by candlelight. "Come closer, son."

Marius obeyed, less because he respected the priest and more because he saw a likely window on the wall behind the man. He might fit through it if he squeezed. The window was made of cut wood, hinged from the top, and held open by a stick.

He ignored the priest, shoving his head out the window.

"That's quite a curse you've got, my son." The priest had a strange way of speaking, as though it were difficult to pull himself out of his thoughts long enough to converse.

Marius pulled his head back in and stared at the priest. "You can see it too?" Marius put a hand to his mouth. "What happened to my stutter?" He hadn't spoken a whole sentence, not counting the limericks, since Asadal had left him for dead.

"I wouldn't be much of a priest if I couldn't abate a curse. Those blasphemous mages and the church are not, ah, exactly best friends these days."

Someone else had referred to wizards as blasphemers. It was Asadal, who had also said that a priest might be able to help him.

"Did you just heal my curse?"

"No. Just abated and, ah, only in my presence. You are cursed in more ways than one, you know. Though you could be entirely healed if you wanted."

Marius wondered what the priest meant.

A sharp knock sounded on the door leading into the room.

"Good Father! Good Father!" It was obviously the plea of a slave for admittance. Shouts followed as the slave reported back to his associates. Marius heard a door smash in. It wasn't theirs. Maybe it was the unhelpful fellow next door. The sound of a scuffle rang out from the hallway. The man had been serious about wanting to see Marcel before he opened the door.

Metal rang against metal. The man must have pulled a sword. Well, thought Marius, assassination attempts are serious business. The longer the man resisted, the better for Marius, and if he just so happened to eat a blade, too bad for him.

"Are you in trouble?" said the priest.

"Father, you don't even know."

Marius stepped onto the bench beside the priest to get a better look out the window. It was a straight drop to the street. The fall looked nasty. Even if he lowered himself by his fingertips as far as he could go, it was still going to be a long fall. If he broke a leg, there was little chance he could escape the city.

He looked left. From the next room over, a nice fat pipe descended to the street. If the man next door had opened up, Marius would have been home free by now.

"Tell me your trouble. I may be able to help." The priest remained seated.

"Weren't you at the banquet?"

"I only stayed for the first course. Protocol and good politics dictate that I, ah, attend these functions. But I do not have to walk in the way of sinners nor sit in the seat of drunkards, as they say. Plus, I heard the night's entertainment was expected to be even poorer than usual."

The man had missed the event of the year. They'd be talking about Marius's performance for months. Even the prince of fools had a fool's pride. But Marius didn't correct the priest.

"I was that entertainment," said Marius. "I'm afraid that I gave offense."

The banging sounded again at the priest's door. It was no longer a weak slave but a strong guard knocking with the pommel of his sword.

"Open the door!"

"Coming!" the priest called out, though he didn't move.

"Father," said Marius. It was time to get serious. He fixed the priest with a look of hope that only a man close to death can muster. "I met a man who said that a priest of Amok could help me."

"Who, pray tell, was that?"

"His name was Asadal," said Marius. "He said that the High Priest of Amok, Campri, might help me. That was just before he left me for dead."

The look on the priest's face changed entirely. He was now extremely awake and aware. He was the one staring at Marius with a hopeful look on his face.

"Asadal is alive? How long ago? When did you see him?"

The priest's outer door was ferociously attacked. They must have two or three big men putting their shoulders into it. The bolt would only hold out so long, and the furniture wouldn't stand a chance against such an assault.

Marius noted the priest's hungry stare and thought he saw a way to bargain.

"Father, I would tell you more. But I'm about to be killed."

"Yes, yes, but about Asadal? He lives?"

"I don't know. Could be." Of course, he didn't add that the old man was being tracked by a crazy Astor.

"Son, I am Campri, and I will help you. Go to the church and hide yourself there. Tell them I sent you. You will be safe for the night. I will come in the morning and, ah, find you safe passage out of the city if you can give me any news of my friend Asadal."

Marius shrugged a shoulder. "Thanks, Father, but how do I get out of this house?"

"Oh, that," said the priest. "Turn around. See that wall beside you. The one with the leering fawn?"

Marius did see the face of the lusty fawn and guessed where the conversation was headed. The eyes of the fawn were peep-holes the gaping mouth hung open in a mocking fashion. Marius shook his head. Nobles were a weird bunch.

He pushed on the wall. A small door opened into the bathroom next door.

"Go through, my son, and, after the pursuit has left, make your way into the street. Wait for me at the church."

"Thank you," said Marius.

The door to the corridor burst open. Marius closed the small hole in the wall and watched through the fawn's leering eyes as the guards rushed in on the priest.

"I'm sorry that I could not get up, good sirs, but these old bowels are, ah, as thick as mortar."

"Father, we're sorry to have disturbed you."

Marius saw a guard check out the window and onto the street below. He called back to his troops.

"The room is empty."

"Blessings, my son, on you."

"Umm, thank you, Father. We'll be leaving you now. Your furniture—"

"God moves in mysterious ways."

"Right. Good night, Father."

Marius saw the priest give a little blessing, moving his hands up and down in front of his chest. After the soldier left, he made the same movement toward Marius, who decided it was time to go.

He stepped onto the bench. It had a hole in the middle, serving as a latrine, emptying out directly onto the street. Marius would not be landing in a pristine garden down there.

He looked through the peep-holes back into the other room. The priest was still there. Marius whispered through the fawn's open mouth.

"Father, one last thing."

"Yes?"

"The magician that was here tonight—"

"Malconus?"

So, that was his name.

"Yes, Malconus. He was the one who cursed me."

"I think not tonight though? Your curse is, ah, too old for that."

"No, it was some time ago. He's after one of the slaves, a girl named Irina. He says she has some gift of healing, of counteracting curses." Marius paused. "She needs help."

"I see," said the priest. "I'll see what I can do."

"Promise me," said Marius. "Or this is the last you'll ever see of me."

The priest paused for a long moment before responding. "We priests do not swear a promise. But I do not lie either. If anything can be done, I will do it. You will simply have to, ah, trust me."

Yeah, thought Marius, as much as I trusted your friend Asadal. Well, it was more assurance than he'd had before. If the priest didn't help, Irina wouldn't survive the next day.

"Thanks, Father."

Marius pulled himself out of the window and slid down the pipe that was mounted to the wall. When he hit the street, his feet were already running toward the church at the heart of Amok.

# Chapter 19

The wooden pew was almost an improvement over the lumpy fruit stall in the market where he usually slept. Marius shifted his head on his bindle. No one had picked up the dirty looking piece of cloth from the alley beside the church. He had regained his worldly possessions, minus his stack of coins, and had lived through the performance at House Marcel. By a Walker's standards, Marius was doing all right.

The view in the sanctuary of the church at dawn was certainly better than the marketplace. The long, narrow building had been designed so that the sun's first rays caught the windows at the front of the church, bathing the images of the Lady in a soft light.

Stone carvings representing the sign of the dove, the sign of the wind, and the sign of the flame, flanked the graceful head of the Lady herself. The three images were said to represent the manifestations of the Lady in the world.

As parishioners filtered into the church for early morning prayers, Marius undid the bindle. He drew the blanket around his head seeking anonymity behind the makeshift hood.

The priest had said he'd be safe in the church. And the doorkeeper, if he was startled at the late night visitor, certainly didn't show it.

The doorkeeper was big, bigger than any man Marius had ever seen. His thick arms had easily and noiselessly moved the heavy wooden doors, allowing Marius entrance. What a church needed with such a muscular specimen, Marius couldn't begin to speculate. Maybe the man had left the army and had taken new orders in the church.

A young priest, not Campri, stood in the front of the church and intoned the morning's prayer, following a centuries-old rite that had supposedly come from the Lady's mouth herself. Hers had been the guiding light that enlightened and led Arovia to prosperity. Marius wondered what the Lady would say, if she even existed, about the current condition of her land. He wondered if she too had owned slaves.

Marius looked around while the priest prayed. The windows of the building were frosted with colors. The sunlight through them was quite inspiring. Each window also had a geometric design built into the iron muntins that separated the individual panes of stained glass. Marius did a double-take. The designs looked almost like Walker signs. There was the bowl shape that signaled rest for the weary and the sign of the table with three loaves that indicated food for the hungry. He didn't recognize all of the signs in the windows.

When the priest finished intoning, he walked down the single aisle between two rows of benches. He stopped and spoke a brief prayer over each of the congregants. When he reached Marius near the back of the church, he said, "Come with me." Marius pulled his eyes away from the stained glass windows.

He followed the priest through a door at the back of the church and into an enclosed courtyard. A grass-covered lawn was marked by burning lamps, the burial markers of the rich. Other graves were marked by wind chimes suspended over the final resting place. The sound was of a thousand small coins hitting stone, a very pleasant sound to a beggar like Marius. Still others were marked by a single low tree, carefully cultivated over time to provide a perch for the birds of the air. Though the arrangement seemed chaotic at first glance, yet as one strolled the path on the lawn, out of the chaos a single image plucked at the mind, such as the sight of a sleeping bird, head tucked beneath its wing or the glint of the sun off of a wind chime.

The overall effect was one of deep peace, even more pleasant than the bath at House Marcel.

Through the walled courtyard, it was a short stroll to the buildings that housed the priests and their families. The young priest led Marius through a large dining room, up a flight of stairs and deposited him into a small waiting chamber. The brawny doorkeeper was standing inside. The priest hurried away on other duties.

The waiting room was sparsely furnished with a bare desk, much too small for the doorkeeper, and a few chairs. But it was lined with books. Hundreds of leather spines of all sizes and colors faced out at Marius. As Marius examined the shelves, the doorkeeper looked Marius up and down.

"Lose the knife," said the doorkeeper. He spoke in a voice that seemed to rise out of the center of the earth to be channeled through the man's cavernous mouth.

"W-w-what?"

"The knife tucked inside your shirt. Take it out. Put it on the table, slowly. And leave the sack too."

Marius had nearly forgotten that he was still carrying the knife he'd used to threaten the wizard Malconus. Carefully withdrawing it from his shirt, mindful of his curse, Marius laid it on the desk. His bindle followed.

"You can step inside now." The man's gruff mannerisms bore none of the young priest's or

Campri's polished refinement. He pointed a meaty thumb toward the entrance to the inner chamber. Marius let himself in.

Campri sat at a desk before a window. The surface of the desk was covered in books as was the floor. It looked as though someone had shaken the shelves like a tree and the books had fallen like leaves around the room.

"Come in," said Campri, absentmindedly. He was deep into a book and had an ink pen poised over the page. "Have a seat."

The chairs were covered in books.

Marius went to move a stack so that he could sit down.

"Oh, my, no," said Campri. He scuttled around the desk, plucking up the stack of books. "Those are carefully arranged, you see." He set them atop another seemingly random pile of books.

"There now," said the old priest, repositioning himself. "Just one moment, please." He made a final note in the book with a flourish before looking up. What was left of his wispy white hair settled light as snow over his forehead. He brushed it back over his balding head. "Continuing our conversation from last night, what can you tell me about Asadal?"

"The girl first," said Marius.

"Ah, yes. I was able to help her. She has, ah, joined the service of the church. It was not easy to get a boon granted by the master of House Marcel today, as you can well understand. But it was done."

"I want to see her."

"In good time, my son."

Marius let out a deep breath. He would have to trust the priest.

"And I want passage out of the city."

"Easily done."

"And I want—"

"My son, in case you didn't realize it, you are in the house of the Lady. You may ask for whatever you like and we will, ah, do as much as we can to aid those in need. This is our duty."

Was it really as easy as all that? He should have come to the church right away, just like Asadal had told him. He might have avoided nearly starving to death and barely escaping punishment as a tomato thief.

Campri said, "Now, please, about Asadal. He is my good friend and I, ah, would know more of him."

Marius told the priest the story of how he and Asadal had met, of how the old man had saved his life and taught him how to survive on the road, and of the ultimate betrayal, leaving him as good as dead in the hands of Lespa as Asadal ran through the woods having stolen Marius's pack.

During the telling, Campri put the points of his fingers together and held them to his mouth.

"And this all happened when?"

"Months ago." He hadn't yet gotten to the part where he wandered the countryside starving before arriving in Amok.

"I take it you blame Asadal for his actions?"

Marius nodded his head. Of course he did. Remembering it now, tears almost came to his eyes. He'd thought of the old man as something more like an uncle.

"Did he ever mistreat you?"

Marius shook his head, no.

"Tell you a lie? Cheat you? Make fun of your curse?"

Marius had to admit at each question that Asadal had done none of those things.

"Yet you assume that, at the final moment of truth, Asadal betrayed you to the Astor?"

Marius nodded.

"Did it ever occur to you that he was protecting you?"

"He left me there to die. She had a knife to my throat."

"Then why didn't she cut it? Lespa is not known for her kindness." The priest removed his hands from his face, placing them in his lap.

"She thought I was a fool, a dupe."

"Why did she think that?"

"Because he took the ring—"

"Which you still insist was an act of betrayal?"

Marius wanted to protest. But the priest caused him to doubt.

"You could not have outrun Lespa yourself. She would have tracked you easily, untrained as you are. And Asadal could not have escaped if he had taken you with him. He did the only thing possible to save you both."

"But he left me alone."

"He told you to find me. If he tried to reconnect with you on the road, Lespa's spies would have found out."

"Asadal stole my bag."

"Ah, yes. That." The priest turned a head, half-looking out the window. "Marius, as a former slave of a lesser house there are things you may not know." He held up a hand, forestalling any hurt feelings by the statement. "Being a slave is no shame. We are all slaves of the Lady." The priest paused. They sat a long time in silence before he continued.

"Arovia is not as peaceful as she may seem. There is a fundamental conflict between the White Tower and the Church of the Lady. We cannot both exist in the heart of the empire. The Lady came to tell us this basic truth. Since her coming, her message has spread and grown into the very church itself. Yet, we are at all times opposed by the White Tower."

The priest's face, normally so very kind, was marred by a frown. Marius sensed the man's distaste for the magicians. It was a feeling Marius shared.

"Do you know the problem with magicians, Marius?"

Marius had a pretty good idea what he thought about a certain mage, Malconus.

"They have power, real power, to do good. Yet they have not used that power to help the poor or those in need. Magic, ah, lies in the ability to manipulate an object or a man's natural traits." The wizard raised an arm, making an imaginary muscle. "They can make a strong man stronger." He pointed to his head, "A smart man smarter. And a womb more womb-like, which is why they are welcomed at weddings."

"Yet they have used their abilities to benefit themselves and, to the extent it serves their interests, the great houses of Arovia."

If the priest had ended the speech with a call to go burn down House Marcel, Marius would have carried the first torch. But he continued.

"Asadal is a spy. Our best. He works for the Lady."

It began to slowly dawn on Marius why a church might need such a big doorkeeper and why he might not be surprised at late night arrivals. There was a war on, and Marius had been caught up in it.

"I tell you all this because it is no secret. The other side knows of Asadal and has hunted him for years. As for your bag, he might have hidden a secret in it. Or he might have taken it to make Lespa think he'd betrayed you."

"But Lespa was after Asadal. And the Astors serve justice for all of Arovia," said Marius.

The priest sighed. "Astors are a law unto themselves. Some are benevolent dictators; some are megalomaniacal lunatics. Lespa is one of the latter. Certainly they, ah, follow what they think is good. But there is only one who is good, the Lady. We must follow her ways."

Marius remembered a similar speech from Asadal.

"That's not all, Marius. Asadal was right to send you to me. There's something strange about you, something about your curse."

Marius had been meaning to ask the priest about that. "You said last night that I was cursed in more ways than one."

"Ah, yes, quite. But I referred then to the wizard's curse and the curse of sin which you bear. In truth, I did think there was something odd about your curse. However, now that I've studied it, I think something beyond the curse is it work."

Campri opened a book, then closed it again. "Yes, something beyond the curse is at work within you. Asadal must have guessed. I think it's why he helped you, took you under his wing. Even I, with all my years of faith can only catch glimpses of it, and only when I'm looking straight at you. You appear, my son, to have been touched by the Lady."

"What do you mean touched?"

"I mean, that she has put her hand on your life."

"I don't believe in the Lady."

"Nevertheless, she sent you aid when you needed it," said Campri. "Tell me. Was a priest nearby when you were cursed?"

"As a matter of fact there was." Much good it had done him.

"I think," said Campri, "that he did what was within his power to help you." Campri stared hard at Marius who flinched under that piercing gaze. "At the same time you were cursed, you were blessed. He asked the Lady to touch you. It is for this reason that when you've been most in need, you have found help."

Marius thought of Asadal and of Irina.

High Priest Campri continued, "You may not be interested in this conflict, but the Lady has taken an interest in you, as has the White Tower. You are at war in your own heart, a war between the wizard's curse and the priest's blessing. Remember, in the end, we must all make a choice."

"What choice?" said Marius. "If the Lady had a hand in my life, if the priest had the power to bless, why did he, why did the Lady, let me get cursed?"

"Perhaps to heal you of your curse." Campri let the news sink in. "If you give your life to the Lady, like Bestius there," he pointed toward the door behind which the big man was standing, "you can be entirely healed. You see, ah, the curse works on your self. If the Lady becomes you, if you join with her, you can be free of the wizard's curse and the curse of your sin. You can be one."

Marius cocked his head back, his eyebrows raised, in a look of incredulity.

"Not now. You don't have to decide now," said Campri. "Think on these things. You could do much good for the Lady if you so choose. Go see your friend. We will talk again before you leave."

Campri returned his attention to the book in front of him as though Marius had never interrupted his deep thoughts.

Marius stood up. He didn't even know how to begin thinking about what Campri had just told him. He looked at the books that had been displaced by his use of the chair, considering whether to replace them. Then he thought better of it. Campri seemed to have a system, though it looked as chaotic as the courtyard outside, there must be some hidden order.

* * *

Downstairs in the dining room sat Irina.

When she saw Marius, she rushed to him with arms outstretched. Her auburn hair bounded off her shoulders. It was everything Marius had ever dreamed of. The curse couldn't ruin this perfectly happy moment.

Besides, the evil magician Malconus had said that Irina had a way of bringing out the good in people. Marius already felt better just for being around her again and especially at having her arms around his neck.

She stepped back, holding his hands.

"Ian told me how you rescued me from that... that man! Thank you, Marius, thank you. And to think how cross I'd been with you, I just—"

"It's o-o-okay." So, her innate talent didn't completely stop the curse. He still stuttered around her. Why couldn't the high priest have come with him so that he could converse with Irina normally for once?

"And the priests told me I have you to thank for my freedom. I'm to serve the church here in Amok. Campri's wife is going to train me. I don't know what to say, Marius." The smile on her face said enough.

"Een?"

A shadow passed across Irina's pretty visage. "He is to remain at House Marcel. I was the only one who got to leave." Then the shadow was gone. "But I can see him often. And his position there is not a bad one. He might even become majordomo one day."

Marius wasn't sure whether to wish his new friend well. It seemed like the majordomo at House Marcel had his hands full. Though, perhaps, like Yavont was rumored to have been, Ian would be more sparing when it came to the beatings.

He sat with Irina in the dining room of the church while Irina regaled him with tales of the night's events as told by the gossipy kitchen staff. To hear her tell it, the story of Prince Pratt of Market Square, his performance and mysterious disappearance, was already the stuff of song and legend.

But to him, he was still Marius and she was Irina. There was one last piece of unfinished business. This was the hardest thing he'd ever done. Performing for House Marcel was cake. Starvation was easy. Facing Lespa paled in comparison.

"Eena," said Marius.

She looked at him with her clever eyes.

"I ul-ul-love you."

She smiled at him. His heart felt as though it would burst.

"Marius, that's so sweet!"

She patted him on the cheek and scooped another spoonful of porridge into her mouth.

* * *

Sweet?

Marius stood in the courtyard with bindle in hand. Campri indicated that he should be ready to leave Amok as soon as night fell. The beauty of the lamp-lit graves, shining through the stained glass baubles that decorated the wind chimes, lent the courtyard a wonderful aura. If he had to die and be buried, he wouldn't mind, if he could be buried someplace like this.

Yet his thoughts kept returning to Irina.

Sweet? It wasn't as though he could stay in Amok to bother her. Not with House Marcel after him. He'd saved her from the wizard and from a life of slavery, yet the best she could do was "Sweet"?

"It's time." Bestius, the doorkeeper put his over-sized paw on the handle of a door leading out into the alley where Marius had stashed his coins. The name fit the man well, thought Marius.

Campri exited the building where the priests and their families lived and worked. He marched purposefully toward Marius.

Campri waved the big ox off a few paces.

"Marius, you've had time to think. Have you decided anything?"

The priest became distracted by some aspect of the courtyard. Marius understood the feeling and waited for him to return his attention to the conversation.

After a time, Marius said, "Much as I want to get rid of the curse, I'm not sure if the price you ask is too high. Asadal held the curse at bay with a piece of grass. Maybe I could learn that trick. Or find someone like Irina. Or I might try to fight it on my own. If I don't use it, don't let it use me, I don't think it can take over."

The priest gave a sad little nod that was totally incongruous with the beatific surrounding.

"I understand, Marius. But if you ever find that you can't do it on your own. Come back. Come back before you, ah, before you become a complete fool."

Marius nodded, sure that the man meant no insult by his choice of phrasing.

"If you will not join the Lady, then I think you should travel to Seatown. Look there for an entertainer named Notori who runs a circus. He will be at the fair in Seatown. Seek him then and there. He might have need of someone with your, ah, particular skills."

"Does he work for the Lady?"

Campri smiled. "You're catching on. But no. Not exactly. Like you, Notori doesn't believe in the Lady, though our interests are aligned. He hates wizards maybe even more than you do."

Marius thought that was hardly likely.

"He may be able to help you manage your curse and your quest."

"My quest?"

"The girl, revenge, redemption, all the usual, ah, stuff of life—or so I've read."

It was Marius's turn to smile. The man had obviously read overmuch, but perhaps, for all that, knew what he was talking about.

"Thank you, Father. Truly."

"I've arranged for a family of loyal tinkers to meet you at the end of the alley. They will escort you out of the city gates. They have so many children, and they come and go so often that one more will not be, ah, noticed," said Campri. "They will help you on the road to Seatown. Go in peace, my son."

"With my curse? Not likely."

Marius let himself out into the alley. He had his bindle, the knife he'd stolen from House Marcel and a few coins given to him courtesy of the church poor box. All in all, not a bad way to start a journey for a Walker.

He met the tinker family and strolled with them and their ox-driven cart out of the gates of Amok. No one recognized him, not with the dirty blanket wrapped around the colorful tunic of Old Huttle's design.

On passing outside of the city walls, Marius paused and asked his friends for a moment alone.

He moved up next to the wall as though he needed to relieve himself. The tinkers looked away.

Instead, crouching down and picking up a rock, Marius scratched a line with three triangles atop it. Underneath, he drew to eyes and a wry smile.

Marius had created a new symbol: the jester's hat. Beneath it he drew an arrow marking the direction of his travel as if to say, here goes the fool, Prince Pratt of Market Square, Marius the Walker, the man with the jester's curse.

## ABOUT THE AUTHOR

Hans Hergot is the pen name of an award-winning author of fantasy and science fiction whose stories convey a redemptive message. Learn more at www.hanshergot.com

The original Hans Hergot lived nearly five hundred years ago. He was a writer, a pamphleteer, and a bookseller who wandered from village to village bringing knowledge and truth. He was burned alive for speaking a wisdom that the world could not understand.

*Deo vindice*

www.ingramcontent.com/pod-product-compliance
Lightning Source LLC
Chambersburg PA
CBHW030305200626
46816CB00002BA/765